Charlotte and the Demons

ALETHEA EASON

Love you,
Alethea

BORDERLAND WRITERS CO-OP

Contents

The Virgin of the Screen Door: 1965

"**M**obsters rule Las Vegas."

Daddy repeated these words so often they became a refrain of my childhood, along with:

"Be on your guard."

"Watch your purses."

"You don't know what's out there. Keep the doors locked."

Daddy worked the vice squad. When he had one too many, he stood in the kitchen, muttering about meat grinders, bodies thrown into Hoover Dam, and how sorry Mommy would be when something happened to him.

His shot glass ~~would~~ clinked on the counter.

Did Mommy or the brass downtown appreciate him?

Hell no.

Clink.

But he did his job.

Clink.

He risked his life.

On days off, he drank pints of Jim Beam and quart bottles of Miller High Life. He watched wrestling matches and country music programs where the sequins on the outfits sparkled as brightly as the lights on Fremont Street.

When he went undercover, Mommy fretted the bad guys would figure out this graying patsy with the crew cut and the LBJ glasses wasn't from Omaha for a convention of insurance salesmen or a down on his luck dentist from Detroit.

Right before fourth grade began, Daddy disappeared for five days, longer than ever before. Through the morning, Mommy cleaned like the white tornado, her dark brown hair in rollers, her face puffy from crying.

My big sister Connie pulled me into her bedroom. Connie's hazel eyes, deep set like Daddy's, darted from my face to her door. "Mom thinks Daddy's been chopped up and buried in the desert halfway to Elko."

Connie echoing Daddy's threats made me twitch inside.

Something crashed in the kitchen. "Sugar foot! Oh beans, oh beans, oh beans!"

I'd bet a bottom dollar Connie's insides were twitchy too because after she'd helped Mommy clean up the shards from the Corningware bowl, I found her in the bathroom pulling out one hair at a time.

Heaviness filled my body. I shuffled to my bedroom to hide away. For some reason, a copy of the *Las Vegas Sun* lay across my bedspread. We weren't subscribers. How did it get there?

The neatly folded paper displayed an article with the headline "Virgin of the Screen Door." A caption "Vasquez Family Claims a Miracle" lay below a picture of a Mexican family standing in front of a modest tract house, a lot like ours. A second picture of the actual door accompanied the article.

We were lapsed Baptists. From what I knew from the few times we went to church, the Virgin didn't count for much. There were no statues of her as in my best friend Rhonda's church. I didn't have a clue about Mary other than her presence in manger scenes at Christmas, but my family needed a miracle. We just had to go see her.

The Vasquez family lived on Acoma Court, not far from us. We could walk there and say prayers for Daddy to come home in one piece. I'd pray extra hard for Mommy to calm down and ask that Connie not go bald.

I ran into the kitchen where Mommy sat on the stool covered in cheery yellow naugahyde, a tissue wadded in her fist.

I shoved the paper in her face. "We need to go to the Virgin."

"What are you talking about, Charlotte?"

I pointed to the picture. "The Virgin Mary. We need to ask her to bring Daddy back."

Mommy took the paper and scanned the article, shaking her head. "This is nonsense."

From Connie's room, the Rolling Stones screamed they weren't getting no satisfaction. Mommy folded the newspaper. She hadn't washed the make-up off her face from the day before, and her powder blue shift looked as though she'd slept in it.

"Turn that down, Connie Louise."

The volume rose.

Mommy sighed and opened the paper again. "Where did you get this?"

I tried to tell her about the newspaper's magical appearance, but she interrupted. "You know what? Going there would be better than stewing in this house. We can get Slurpees on the way back." She reached up and unsnapped a roller. A tendril of dark hair flopped over her ear. "Tell Connie we're leaving in a few minutes."

I wadded into Connie's room and shouted over the music. Connie rolled her eyes, but the promise of Slurpees persuaded her to turn off the record player.

We hadn't gone halfway before the heat of the sidewalks rose through the rubber soles of my sneakers. Maybe this mission wasn't such a good idea.

We passed the 7-11.

Mommy read our minds. "On the way back, girls. We're on a pilgrimage."

Connie's cheeks turned crimson. "This is so stupid. I don't even believe in God."

God being an option had never occurred to me. Connie's flip-flops snapped against the soles of her feet. My sister suddenly felt distant, a being to herself born out of the shimmering heat of the asphalt.

Mommy ignored Connie, but took my hand and held it until both of ours grew slippery with sweat. Mine fell out of hers. We walked in silence until we reached Acoma Court, a cul de sac of small stucco houses with drapes drawn to keep out the heat. A weary looking St. Bernard barked unenthusiastically behind a cinder block fence.

Sweat ringed Connie's hairline. "If you weren't afraid of driving, we'd have been here and back, Mother."

"Well, we're here now."

Three old women knelt in front of the porch, the shadows from the eaves partially shading them. Five other women of various ages sat on lawn chairs under a large umbrella talking in Spanish to a young priest with bright red hair and a florid face. A couple of toddlers splashed in a wading pool beneath another umbrella decorated with ducks. Several empty chairs were set up in the yard.

A young boy with a buzz cut and long eyelashes offered us glasses of lemonade. Connie and I drank greedily and squashed our cups, throwing them into the grocery bag under the table. Mommy stood behind the praying women and twisted a handkerchief she'd pulled from her purse.

A gold Impala pulled up to the house. An old black couple emerged slowly from the sedan. The boy ran to them, took the wife's arm, and led her to a chair. The husband sat next to her with wheezing breaths. Her purse unlatched with a click. She opened it and took out foldable fans for both of them.

A large woman about Mommy's age looked at her watch and pulled towels from a pink plastic laundry basket on the ground next to her. She walked over in an uneven gait and offered them to us.

"For your knees."

Mommy motioned for us to take one. "Don't be rude, girls. Say thank you."

Despite her earlier protests, Connie took a towel, knelt and clasped her hands. I joined her and stared at a stain on the screen that looked like the whorls in the fleshy part of my thumb. While we knelt, a fluffy cloud grew overhead, shading the little congregation from the three p.m. sun. My knees started to hurt. Connie had spoken the truth, coming here was a dumb idea.

The seated women suddenly dropped to their knees and crossed themselves vigorously.

The old couple lifted their arms. "Praise, Jesus!"

I glanced at Connie. She stared intently and frowned. Next to her, Mommy squeezed her eyes so tightly little wrinkles creased her cheeks. Turning back to the screen, I softened mine the way I did when I tried to see animals in the clouds while a thunderstorm gathered.

A young woman's brown face slowly formed in the middle of a whorl. A royal blue veil flowed like a waterfall from the top of her black hair to the aluminum filigree at the bottom of the screen. The veil opened to reveal she wore a silver miniskirt. White go-go boots clad her holy feet. She caught my eyes with her obsidian ones, winked, and then faded back into the thumbprint.

Recitations of Hail Mary's intensified like a swarm of bees leaving a hive. The old couple began to shout in the strangest language, words that sounded ancient, full of flowing syllables, in a cadence making their utterances clear and sharp.

More cars drove up Acoma Court. Glancing over my shoulder, a VW bug with peeling paint, a white pickup, and a dark green sedan were parking in a line. Doors flung open. Families in their Sunday best poured out, men and boys in suits and ties, little girls with frilly dresses, and women with pure white veils floating like clouds over straps of sundresses.

The children must have been warned to be on their best behavior because they walked quietly from the cars to the boy with lemonade. No jostling. No laughing. But clearly, the lemonade, not the screen door, interested them the most. I recognized a girl who'd be starting sixth grade at my school. She didn't look my way.

The three men bent down, each on one knee. A couple of the women grasped their hands in a *here is the church, here is the steeple, open the door, where's all the people* style. The others made prayer hands like the pictures I'd seen on billboards about needing to be saved, or else.

My private visitation had vanished and whispers surrounded me.

"Oh, there she is."

"Blessed are you among women."

And weeping, weeping, weeping. The Vasquez family were prepared with tissues and passed them out. The young priest held the hands of a sobbing grandmother.

Mommy stood up and straightened the skirt and blouse she'd put on before we left. She slowly looked around and crossed her arms. Connie joined her. The old couple's strange praise grew louder. Connie started to laugh, but Mommy shushed her and beckoned me with her index finger. Her lips formed the words, "Let's go."

An image filled my head of Daddy blowing on a pair of dice, his other hand holding a cigar. Gangsters with fedoras pulled low over their faces circled the table, hands twitching next to their bulging coat pockets where their pistols waited to be fired.

I turned back to the door and whispered as fast as possible, "Please, JesusMaryGod, let Daddy be safe. Let Connie stop pulling her hair out so she can be popular. That's what she wants more than anything. Let Mommy not worry so much."

The picture of the guardian angel that hung over Rhonda's bed replaced Daddy's image. The angel looked like a fairy in her sky blue dress and wings the color of opals, my birthstone. She floated behind a little boy and girl crossing a bridge. I needed a guardian angel badly. I didn't think it fair we Baptists didn't get them.

"And, JesusMaryGod, send me an angel. Please, please, please."

"You got it, kiddo."

My eyes popped open. Mary's face emerged from the screen in the same way Porky Pig's did at the end of cartoons. I expected her to say, "That's all folks," but instead she gave me a thumbs up and disappeared again.

Mommy stood behind me. "Get up, Charlotte."

Cars now filled Acoma Court. The people who arrived first would have a hard time leaving if they wanted to. We wove through the crowd to the stop sign at the corner, leaving the miracle behind.

A car full of nuns passed by. They waved at us.

Mommy wiggled her fingers at them. "Don't tell your Daddy we came here. He wouldn't like it."

Connie shook something from one of her flip-flops. "What a waste of time."

They hadn't seen her? I began to cry.

Mommy touched my face. "What's wrong, sweetheart?"

"Mary had on go-go boots. And she talked to me."

Mommy pulled her hand away. "You're too old to tell stories, Charlotte."

Connie chimed in. "Yeah, Charlotte."

Mommy clutched her purse tightly to her side. "Let's get those Slurpees."

She marched off in front of us.

The moment we walked in the house, Connie hightailed it to her room.

I followed and leaned against her door frame. "I really did see Mary."

She collapsed on the bed and covered her face with her arms. "Leave me alone."

Daddy returned around seven o'clock. He hadn't been whacked by the mob. My prayer had been answered. Best of all, he carried a grocery bag tucked in his arm, set it on the counter, and pulled out a container of strawberry ice cream. He'd also shopped for a pint of Jim Beam and placed the bottle next to it.

He drew me to his side for a hug. "How about a milkshake?" Tobacco and a filmy scent of stale booze infused his polo shirt. He opened a cabinet under the counter and looked inside. "June, where's the blender?"

Mom shuffled into the kitchen in her pink house shoes. "Why didn't you call to let us know you were alive? Do you have any idea how worried we were? Isn't that right, Charlotte? The blender is right there behind the Tupperware. It could bite you."

Daddy took it out and got the scoop from the drawer above the cabinet. I stepped backward until I bumped the dining table.

Mommy stepped so she was only a couple of inches behind Daddy. "You didn't even come straight home, did you? You had to stop at a filthy bar. You were probably drunk the whole time you were on the job."

Daddy's big back froze. "Stop breathing down my neck, June."

"Talk to me, Walter."

Daddy slammed the scoop down. Pink ice cream flew to the wall behind the blender. He grabbed the whisky bottle. Shoving Mommy aside, he stormed through the living room and out the sliding glass door to the patio.

The scent of strawberry lingered in the kitchen. A hush fell, balanced on pins and needles. Mommy quietly opened the fridge. Out came the eggs and milk. She cracked an egg into the blender, poured in the milk, and turned it on. My insides felt like they were being mixed up along with shake. She turned it off, poured my treat into one of our most generous glasses and handed it to me.

"There you go."

She made a beeline to the patio. The shake slipped sweet and thick over my tongue.

Later, Connie and I held each other on her bed as our parents battled in the living room. A thud hit the wall. Mommy rushed into the bathroom. We eased ourselves into the hallway. She leaned over the sink, pressing a wash rag over her left temple. Connie pulled me back into her room.

⇒⇒⇒〉 〈⇐⇐⇐

I must have woken up after midnight because the TV shows were over for the night. Static from our set traveled to my bedroom, layering itself over the silent gulf left from my parent's fight.

In the dark, a small flame ignited and died. The subtle odor of sulfur wafted to me. A young man leaned against my closet door wearing a black leather jacket like the juvenile delinquents in the old movies my mother watched in the afternoons.

I pulled the covers over my head.

"Sorry to scare you, Cupcake, I really am, but there isn't any other way to show up."

His voice was soft like the red velvet dress I'd worn the previous Christmas. I peeked out. His slight build and wavy black hair made me think of Little Joe Cartwright. *Bonanza* was in black and white at my house, but my apparition appeared in living color. A halo glowed above his head, soft and muted like my nightlight.

"You're the angel God sent me?" I sat up. "You're a boy. I wanted a girl angel."

He pulled two decks of cards like the ones Daddy used for poker from the inside pocket of his jacket. "Sorry to disappoint."

He dropped a card and bent to pick it up. Red horns poked from his head, sprouting a couple of inches above his ears and sprinkled with what looked like silver glitter. They supported his halo and caught its light. Sparks of light shot across to me and fell in silence, evaporating around me like snowflakes.

I scooted into the corner behind my bed. "Angels don't have horns."

He continued shuffling. "I'm going to be straight with you. I'm not an angel."

Strawberry flavored bile rose into my throat. Blood rushed from my legs and arms. Sweat covered my skin and I grew chilled.

"I'm going to call Daddy."

"Hey, calm down." He sat on the rug and began to lay the cards face down. "We both know he's passed out, and we both know that's not fair. Part of the reason I'm here, Charlotte."

He scattered cards over the carpet. I pushed myself back into the corner.

"How do you know my name?"

My visitor raised his head. He didn't smile to make me feel better. "I know everything about you, Cupcake. What a good girl you're trying to be. You love to draw, right?"

I nodded.

He leaned back and put his hands on his knees. "My name is Ezequiel. I'm not going to hurt you, and I promise to explain everything in time. Do you like to play Concentration?"

I nodded again.

He opened his hands toward me. "Then you go first."

I pushed the covers back with my feet, slid to the floor, and turned the card closest to my bed. Red seven of hearts. I picked the card to its left. Black seven of hearts.

"You put the newspaper on the bed, didn't you?"

"Yep. My boss wanted your family out of the house for a while. I hoped you'd get a blessing, but Lily changed the channel from Heaven to—the other place."

His boss? The other place? I stared at the cards. "I didn't see the Virgin?"

Ezequiel picked a red ace of hearts and a black three of spades. "No, but the other people who believe in Mary thought they did. She and Lily have a connection."

I turned over a new card with a lump in my throat. Black five of diamonds. I stared at the pattern the diamonds made for a moment and got on my knees. I reached for a card in the middle of the room. Red five of diamonds.

"Who's Lily?"

Ezequiel rose and opened my closet. "Someone who used to own these go-go boots."

He stepped away. I forced myself to look up. The boots perched below my clothes, white and perfect. I jumped to my feet, hopped across the cards and grabbed them.

I held them to my chest. "Rhonda got some last week, but Mommy said we can't afford them."

He finally smiled. "She won't notice you're wearing them."

I slipped the boots on. They fit perfectly.

We played in silence until I had 52 matched pairs stacked around me. I handed the decks back to Ezequiel. He put them back into his jacket. He looked like an ordinary thin teenage boy, if you didn't notice the halo and horns.

"So, are you a guardian devil?"

He scoffed. "Heck no, I'm not even a demon, only an underling who does the filing. I came across an item detailing a caper going down in Vegas that involves your house. I volunteered to be on a team so I'd have a chance to watch out for you. If the boss accepts me, I plan to work undercover like your dad." He glanced back at my closet. "Only, I won't have the LVPD as back up."

This kid thought he'd protect me?

"What's going to happen, Ezequiel?"

"Nothing to you, I promise. I'll make sure of it."

The TV turned off. Daddy had woken up.

Ezequiel glanced at the dark space in front of my door. "I'll see you tomorrow night."

He stepped into my closet, smashing my clothes behind his back. He took a match I hadn't noticed from behind his ear and scratched it on the bottom of his shoe. A spark flared and died.

The recliner squeaked as Daddy got out of it. I kicked off my new boots and scrambled into bed. A faint odor of liquor hit my nose as he paused in front of my opened door. He muttered something before he wavered down the hall to Mommy.

⇛⇛ ⇚⇚

The next morning the boots lay where I'd flung them. Would Mommy really not see them? Only one way to find out. I wore them beneath my nightgown at breakfast. No one said a word, not even Connie.

I walked over to Rhonda's that afternoon. A doctor had put her on a diet. Mommy described her now as pleasantly plump and praised her peaches-and-cream complexion. Millie, Rhonda's mother, said we were like Mutt and Jeff, whoever they were, light and dark, tall and short.

We played *Bonanza* in the backyard, pretending her swings were horses. I itched to tell her about Ezequiel, but she'd call me crazy. So I mentioned the other thing on my mind.

"You have to be Hoss's girlfriend."

Rhonda put her feet out and stopped her swing. "I'm not going to be his girlfriend. You're going to be his girlfriend."

I knew she'd fight me on this, so I'd prepared myself with my almost nine-year-old logic. "But Hoss and I don't match. Both you and Hoss are pleasantly plump. Little Joe is little—like me."

Rhonda bolted from the swing. "I'm going to tell my mom you said I'm fat."

I jumped off mine. "Okay, you take Adam."

"Adam's not on the show anymore. Besides, he's old. Little Joe is going to be my boyfriend. You have to take either Hoss or Hop Sing."

"You can't have Little Joe because my guardian demon looks like him." My hand shot up to cover my mouth.

Rhonda's fair complexion turned paler. "Did you say demon?"

"Actually, he's an underling." I sat back down and let my feet dangle. "He visited me last night after we went to the Virgin yesterday."

Rhonda got know-it-all on me. "At the Vasquez's? Mom says it's a bunch of hooey."

"Well, it isn't. But Mary didn't show up. Somebody named Lily did, and she talked to me. And then Ezequiel came last night, and we played Concentration. I got every match on the first try. I swear I did."

"Are you feeling okay, Charlotte?"

I didn't answer her, and I didn't say a word about my parents' fight. Mommy didn't allow me to talk about what happened at home to anyone, but she did tell me Rhonda's dad punched a hole through a wall and took a swing at Millé. That's when she divorced him. Mommy warned me if I ever brought up what had happened between Rhonda's parents, I'd be in big trouble. The McCauley's were Catholic. Being divorced was very, very bad for them.

Millie worked in the office at a car dealership. Mommy admired her doing this. Daddy told her not to get any big ideas.

Rhonda joined me back on the swing set and twirled in her seat, winding the chain. She picked up her feet and spun around. I pushed myself toward the bars so she wouldn't hit me.

"I'm telling the truth. Lily even had him bring me invisible go-go boots."

Why did I have to mention the boots?

Rhonda planted her feet below the swing. "They're not invisible, Charlotte. They look like mine. But your mom said she wasn't buying any. What changed her mind?"

Millie opened the sliding glass door and stepped out. "Hour's up. Time to head home."

Rhonda, of course, tattled on me. "Charlotte says her boots are invisible and someone named Lily gave them to her."

Millie smiled like she wasn't getting a joke. "Those are the best boots I've never seen. Actually, Charlotte, I've been meaning to ask you where you got your sandals. They're adorable."

Now I had to lie. "Tom Mcan. We always get our shoes there."

⇛⇛⇛ ⇚⇚⇚

Ezequiel visited me every night. At first, we didn't talk about scary things but played games. I always won. Sometimes he told me stories or sang "La Bamba" softly in Spanish.

One night before school started, Ezequiel taught me strategies for Chinese Checkers so I could beat Connie. A thunderstorm brewing that afternoon finally let go during our second game. Rain pelted the house and flashes of lightning lit my room every minute or so.

After an especially close strike, thunder engulfed the house. Ezequiel glanced at my closet and then grabbed a handful of marbles, throwing them into the game box. "I don't feel like playing anymore, Cupcake."

I tried a strategy that worked the week before when he'd lost interest in Mousetrap. I cocked my head and put on a fake pout. "Pleeeeeese, Ezequiel."

He finished picking up the game and closed the lid. "Not tonight. I've put off talking to you about the serious stuff, Charlotte. I can't wait anymore."

My stomach felt like a brick had been dropped inside it. I grabbed a pillow from my bed and hugged it as I sat cross-legged in front of him. "About the other place?"

He scooted so his back pressed against my closet door, "Sorry, Charlotte. I need to explain why I've come."

Shuffling sounds and groans filtered into my room, followed by a loud bang.

I pointed to my closet with a shaking finger. "Your boss is in there?"

"No, underlings and goons moving equipment around. They're not in your closet, but on the underside of it. I'm pretty sure there's still some time before transport."

I pulled my pillow off my bed and buried my head in it.

"Hey, you're going to be okay, but can you sleep in Connie's room from now on?"

I came up for a breath. "Are you kidding me?"

Daddy was working at the precinct headquarters that night. Somehow Mom and Connie slept through the storm. The cell passed, and now the rain quietly patted my window. The house seemed to breathe in and out with me.

Ezequiel eyes caught mine like a tractor beam. "I left Earth in 1952. I grew up in a little town in New Mexico called Lordsburg. My brother had gone into the Air Force, stationed in Germany. I got my license. Levi's Chevy Coupe had been in our front yard for almost a year. So I borrowed it, and my friend Hector borrowed his dad's Ford F-1. We wanted to have fun. We raced out in the desert, but I lost control of Levi's car."

I squeezed my pillow tighter. "That's why you went to Hell?"

We sat a long time in the glow of my nightlight and his halo.

He stretched out his right leg. "No, that's not why. My little sister Joanne saw me take the keys from the hook in the kitchen. She said she'd tell my parents if I didn't take her with me. She was Connie's age."

I needed a minute to understand what he meant. "Did she go to Hell too?"

Ezequiel bowed his head. "Oh, no, but I took her life, Charlotte. I've been dead almost thirteen years, and I'm still in high school and working a boring job. The worst part is Drivers Ed. I've watched a movie of the accident ten thousand times by now. I keep telling myself I'm going to look away, but when the teacher turns on the projector I can't stop staring. I'm thrown against the steering wheel. Joanne —"

He wrapped his arms around himself. "I didn't protect Joanne, but I'm going to take care of you. Next time I come—"

I didn't let him finish. I didn't want to think about next time. "Why do you have a halo?"

He didn't answer. Glittery sparks flew from his horns, their embers dying before they reached the floor. I crawled over and reached for the glowing circle above his head. He jerked it away, but ~~the tips of~~ my fingertips sizzled.

Daddy's car pulled into the driveway. Headlights flashed in my room the way the lightning had. Ezequiel struck a match and disappeared.

Brother

On the first day of school, every fourth grade girl skipped onto the playground in sparkling white go-go boots. I wore mine proudly as I lined up on the blacktop with my classmates. The hundred plus degrees predicted for the afternoon hovered on the outskirts of the warm morning. The sky above Hannah Clapp Elementary stretched above our heads the same clear blue as chlorinated water in a swimming pool.

Our principal, Mr. Willowby, marched from the teachers' room with the twenty-one Clapp teachers, in order from kindergarten to sixth grade. Out of earshot of Daddy, Mommy referred to Mr. Willowby as "Fred MacMurray." Pipe smoke often wafted from his office onto the walkway to the cafeteria. When winter came on, he dressed in tweed jackets with patches on the sleeves. Today, he wore the standard Las Vegas professional summer attire for men: a crisp white short-sleeved dress shirt, tan slacks, and a thin dark blue tie.

Mr. Olivera, my teacher, waved at us with a big welcome grin in the middle of the string of women instructors. He was bald other than a fringe of salt and pepper running along the back of his scalp from ear to ear. He dressed in the white-shirt-tan-pants uniform but also donned a red and white polka dot bow tie. Connie, who'd been in his class three years before, told me he wore a different one for every day of the week. Kind of like our days-of-the-week underwear we got in our 1963 Christmas stockings, except he never mixed up the days like we did. The polka dot tie belonged to Tuesdays, fitting for the day after Labor Day.

Chatter settled down. Tommy Shelton, last year's student body vice president and now president pro-temp until new elections, held the flag to the right of Mr. Willowby. He had a reedy voice. It was hard to hear his "Ready. Salute."

I put my hand on my heart.

My class would be called the Lucky 13s, named after our room number. Rhonda's class, the Responsible 14s, stood to our left, and to my right, the Respectful 12s. I appreciated how the odds played out for me. I preferred being lucky, rather than being respectful or responsible any day of the week. I had a whole year of good fortune to look forward to.

Rhonda's hair balanced on her shoulders in an upturned curl of gold. I bet Millie must have used a half a can of Aqua Net to achieve such perfection. After repeating "with liberty and justice for all," we waved at each other. We'd put our squabble over Little Joe behind us, coming to the conclusion over the previous weekend Paul McCartney beat Little Joe in the cute department, and vowed with a serious pinky swear we'd never fight over a Beatle.

To keep our bargain safe, I didn't share the daydream that played in my mind about Paul when "Yesterday" came on the radio. Paul would tell me how groovy I looked in my new boots, and then we'd take a ride on a double decker bus. I was 17, like in the song, and when we'd finished touring London, he'd kissed me.

I hadn't mentioned Ezequiel again. Rhonda never commented about my strange remarks that day in her backyard. If she thought I'd gone temporarily loco, so be it.

Only one thing didn't seem right. Ezequiel hadn't returned since the night he'd told me about his sister. I'd rub the rough skin that had healed over the burns on my fingertips to prove to myself he'd been real. Every night before I went to bed, I checked my closet to be sure no fissures to Hell had opened. I tried to stay awake in case he might show up, but I always drifted into a deep sleep before nine o'clock.

Daddy had rotated to the swing shift, working at headquarters for the next couple of months, laying low to take his profile off the streets for a while. I woke to his snoring every morning. I only saw him on his days off because he left before I came home from school. He and Mommy squabbled, but they didn't get into any knock down drag outs during this period.

Mr. Olivera put me into the Road Runner reading group. We didn't have the status of the Jack Rabbits, the top group, but I'd been an Iguana the whole year in third grade. Life was looking up!

But the very best thing was Connie running for seventh grade student body president. My sister brimmed with confidence. Mommy complimented her on her cheerful demeanor more than once. On October 4th, the day before my birthday, Connie won class presidency by a unanimous vote, blossoming overnight into the most popular girl of Dwight Eisenhower Junior High.

My prayer for my sister had come down the pike.

Connie crowed over dinner. "This year's class president, next year the cheerleading team, and in ninth grade, I'm going to be crowned the Spring Dance Queen."

Mommy wiped a smudge of spaghetti sauce from the edge of her mouth. "Your daddy won't let you go to dances, you know that. Not at fourteen, which you will be in ninth grade. And I have no way to take you to away games."

Connie chopped her spaghetti into chunks with her fork. "I'd travel on the bus with the team."

That would go over like a lead balloon. "With the boys? Not likely."

"Charlotte, don't talk with your mouth full." Mommy's attention switched back to my sister. "How would I pick you up at school after you got back from the games?"

Connie's head bent so low, her light brown hair almost covered her plate. "You need to learn to drive."

We had a moment of silence. Daddy once tried to show Mommy how to back out of the driveway. She plowed into the mailbox, and her driving career was history.

Mommy changed the subject. "How short are the skirts?"

Connie pushed her chair from the table. "You should be happy for me."

Mommy put down her fork. "I am so proud of you, Connie Louise, I could burst."

Why didn't she ever call me Charlotte Marie? There were things about my family I would never fathom.

She rose and walked around the table, knelt next to Connie's chair, and took her hands. "The first president in the Johnson family."

Daddy didn't let us forget Andrew Jackson was a cousin, the hero of the Battle of New Orleans, the seventh president of the United States, and the first one who wasn't a sissy.

I swirled spaghetti around with my fork only to watch it fall off. "What about Old Hickory?"

Mommy shot me a mind-your-own-business look. "Well, then, the first female president in the family. I think we should call Grandma and tell her the good news, don't you?"

Mommy carried our plates to the sink and then picked up the phone to dial Indiana.

Connie grudgingly obeyed when Mommy motioned for her to take the receiver. She wrapped the telephone cord around her fingers. "Hi, Grandma. I hope it isn't too late back there. Guess what?"

I slipped away to my room and discovered Ezequiel leaning over my desk examining pictures of horses I'd drawn.

He picked up a picture of a palomino. "Not bad."

Putting my finger to my lips, I closed my door. I turned on the Herman Hermits album I'd left on my turntable. "Where have you been?"

He smiled impishly. "I have an early birthday present." He pulled a ball point pen from his pocket. "Think of a color and click. You can draw with red, black, turquoise, chartreuse, you name it. And it will never run out of ink."

Connie's voice rose in excitement as she let Grandma know about her wonderful life. I inched up the volume on "I'm Henry the VIII, I Am" to drown her out. The pen was a wonder to behold. I would never get a better gift in my whole life, but what if Mommy heard us?

"You shouldn't be here right now."

Ezequiel ignored me, took off his jacket, and hung it on the back of my desk chair. He had rolled up a pack of cigarettes in his shirt sleeve. "This is the only time I had the chance to get away."

I crossed my arms in disappointment. "Cigarettes are bad for you."

He touched the pack. "They're only for show. I'm the only underling in the history of Hell to arrive with a halo. I have to do something to look tough." He sat on top of my desk. "And how is Madame President?"

I placed my hands on my hips. "Did you have anything to do with her election?"

"Who me?" He looked up at the ceiling in feigned innocence. "Well, there are a few perks in working in the filing department. I made a tiny alteration in Connie's paperwork."

I hopped on the desk next to him. We both just fit. "Rhonda's brother, Jason, tickles Rhonda until she cries." I leaned my head on his cigarette pack. "You're a much better brother. I've missed you."

"I've missed you too, Cupcake. Do you really think of me like that?"

I clicked my pen and drew a heart at the base of my thumb in the aquamarine shade of Mommy's jewelry box. "Yep, but I have a question. Since you've been gone, I've been wondering about something. Is there some sort of telephone connection between Heaven and Hell?" I pointed to the ceiling. "I prayed in that direction."

"Ever watch *Get Smart*?" Ezequiel took off his well-worn black loafer and pretended to talk in it. I giggled, and he slipped it back on. "Seriously, Charlotte?"

I let out the breath I didn't know I'd been holding. "Yes, seriously."

"Truth is, I don't know. Remember when I said Mary and Lily had a connection? There's some kind of communication that goes on. The On-High—"

"Who?"

"God prefers being called the On-High. Anyway, rumor has it the On-High keeps close tabs on what goes on in Hell." He stood and took a rolled-up piece of beige paper from the back pocket of his pants. "In case you're wondering, nothing has ever filtered down to me from Upstairs."

My bottom lip trembled. "It'd be nice if it had."

"Hey, chin up." He unfurled the paper. "Good news. I've graduated. My diploma, Cupcake."

I scooted off the desk and leaned back against it. "No more Drivers Ed?"

"Nope." He grinned widely. "I finally made myself look away from the movie."

I took the diploma from him. Ezequiel's name was printed in large black letters and beneath it *Underling First Class* written in an ornate cursive. At the bottom, a mark had been burned into the paper like a brand the Cartwrights might use on their cattle.

"My boss said he's going to hire me for the job. I can watch out for you now." Ezequiel took the diploma and put it back in his pocket. "I might make Demon Third Class in half a century or so, if they don't find what I'm up to."

The phone call must have ended. Mommy yelled from the kitchen. "Charlotte, get in here and help with the dishes."

I shouted over the Hermits. "I'll be right there."

I didn't like thinking about Ezequiel becoming a demon. I did a quick calculation. In half a century, I'd be 59. Well, I wouldn't worry about what might happen when I'd be old, old, old.

"Do you get a paycheck?"

"No, but I have air conditioning now. What a relief."

~~Being a lifelong Las Vegan~~ Having lived my whole life in Las Vegas, I understood the importance of that particular perk.

Ezequiel's face suddenly clouded. I'd been in the presence of sunshine and now a storm had descended.

"What's wrong?"

He looked down for a moment. When his gaze returned to me, his irises flickered with tiny flames. They were beautiful.

"There's something I need to show you."

He guided me by the shoulder to my closet and slid the fake wood panel of the right door behind the left. Hot air slammed against my face. My shoes were piled in the corner. A gap took the place of where the floor had been.

"Your Hell door has gotten big enough for transports to start soon. If you ever are awake when they come, I want you to promise me you won't scream. Pretend you're asleep."

"You're scaring me."

Mommy yelled from the kitchen again. "Do I have to drag you out of your room?"

Ezequiel spoke fast. "There's a bit of time before the transport begins, but you need to prepare yourself for when the job goes down. If you hear my voice, don't say anything. If my boss knew I'm helping you, I'd be in big trouble. No one down there cares that Hell is full of a bunch of bullies, but I do."

What power did he have to help me? He was just a teenager.

"Why do you care so much?"

Ezequiel pointed to his halo. "Maybe because of this thing. Go help your mother. I don't want to be late for work."

He didn't light a match this time to disappear. He simply stepped into the abyss. I watched him fall through the heat before the floor closed over his head.

I tried my best to spend nights with Connie. I even offered to take the floor, but as I suspected she'd have none of it. When I asked Mommy if I might sleep with her and Daddy, she said big girls slept alone and bad dreams couldn't hurt me. She gave me a bell to ring if I got scared. She'd come in and check on me.

A lot of luck that would do with demons breaking in.

I laid in bed afraid to breathe each night until sleep overcame me. I'd never been a scaredy cat in the dark, but now I was afraid of the shadows, the strange shapes my stuffed animals and my piggy bank assumed on the ledge above my desk, the folds in my curtains, the menace of my closet doors.

When would the Hell door open? And what would I see? Would Ezequiel be there when they did?

Night after night nothing happened.

But then, on the night of November 11th—I remember the date because I hadn't gone to school because of Veterans' Day—Ezequiel walked out, and he wasn't alone.

He must have seen I was awake. He barely shook his head and moved his index finger back and forth with the tiniest gesture. I closed my eyelids halfway. Ezequiel faced the closet, squatted, and pulled out something heavy. A figure about twice his size grunted as he pushed the object from the other end.

They passed by my bed carrying a slot machine. Ezequiel's companion seemed to be dragging a foot. He had a hood on, so I didn't see his face, but his fingers were way too long to be human. A slurping accompanied each of his steps, as though his feet were made of slime.

Out my door they went. Their footsteps vanished into silence. I lay paralyzed until my left arm beneath me started to fall asleep. I turned to my stomach and felt the pricking of needles as it came back to life. Ezequiel and his partner returned, stepped into the closet and pulled out another slot machine.

By the fourth trip, I relaxed, more fascinated than scared. I fell asleep after they passed me the fifth time, rolling a poker table.

The Saturday before Thanksgiving, the Dwight Eisenhower Junior High School student council put on the Harvest Festival. Connie had been phoning her friends for a week, telling them what to do in a bossy voice that would have made me furious, yet friend after friend came through for her.

Connie told me if I insisted on wearing a costume for the fair, I had to be a turkey. Mommy had sewn Connie's Pilgrim dress the week before. I wasn't thrilled about having to be the main course.

I wanted a dress like hers, but Connie laid down the law. "No way, José. I'm not going to show up with a copycat little sister. Dig out those construction paper feathers you did in first grade."

Well, wearing a turkey costume would be better than not having one at all. Mommy had saved some of our art projects in the bottom shelf of her hutch in the living room. I found the turkey hat underneath a pile of finger paintings with cracked paint. The headband that fit my six-year-old head had torn in two and the feathers hung limp like they'd molted.

Mommy sat down in the brown recliner holding one of Daddy's shirts and her sewing kit. "What are you doing, Doll Baby?"

She put her work on the table next to the chair and eased down beside me. She picked up the piece of construction paper from kindergarten where I'd drawn my hand-prints and then took my right hand and placed it on top.

"Only yesterday you were that little."

I held up the miserable feathers so she'd see them. "Connie said I have to be a turkey."

"Don't mind your big sister. I have some leftover material. I can make you a dress for tomorrow, if you want. You can be an honorary pilgrim from Clapp Elementary."

Connie overheard us from the kitchen. "Forget about it, Mom. Only the student council are allowed to be Pilgrims."

Fortunately, the telephone rang. Connie got busy bossing a friend on the other end about the exact number of drops of red and yellow food coloring needed to make the specific shade of orange she wanted the cookies to be.

By the next morning, Connie seemed to forget she'd been upset, but her change in attitude probably had a lot to do with Daddy having the day off. He helped her build a five foot long cornucopia out of chicken wire and brown wrapping paper. In the afternoon, he secured it with ropes in the trunk of his LTD where it hung over the back end of the car. In the back seat, he strapped a tank the pet store loaned for the event loaded with fifty donated goldfish in plastic bags filled with water, prizes for the cornucopia bean bag toss.

Daddy had only downed four beers when he and Connie left for school, an excellent sign he'd be more or less not drunk by the evening. He'd return after he helped set things up.

As soon as they'd left, Mommy drummed her fingers on the counter and looked out at the distance. "Should I pour a little of the whiskey down the drain? He might notice it's watered down. But I know he's going to want a kicker for the festival."

I wished she'd kept her fretting to herself. Her words cast a net of pins and needles over me, and I knew she didn't want me to give her my two-cents of leaving well enough alone. To distract myself, I drew pictures of Rhonda and me riding horses with silver manes at the kitchen table, then sketched Ezequiel's face in the corner of the paper.

Mommy bent down to look. "He looks like Little Joe."

Mom finally took the whiskey out of the cabinet. Then, puffing out her breath, she'd set the bottle on the counter, glancing at the clock. Finally, she tipped about a quarter of the contents into the sink as Daddy's car hummed into the driveway.

"Oh, beans."

She filled the bottle, shook it, placed it back in the cabinet, and poured out the morning coffee left in the percolator.

Mom fanned the air. "I hope that will mask the whiskey smell."

About five heartbeats later, Daddy stepped in with a paper bag. He'd taken a side trip to the liquor store and bought three more quarts of beer. He might not hit the whiskey, or if he did, he'd be already too drunk to notice Mommy had doctored it.

A win-win, right? Well, he had to drive us to the carnival either way.

Amber bubbles fizzed to the top of Daddy's beer glass as he sat down at the table. He pointed to Ezequiel's face. "Who's that?"

I imagined a gold halo and clicked my pen.

"An angel." I colored in the halo and put the pen down. I hated being watched when I drew. "Do you want to play Chinese Checkers, Daddy?"

He took a sip from his beer glass and gave me a big smile. "Does the Golden Nugget have slot machines?"

I hoped not the ones Ezequiel had brought from Hell.

I rushed to my room because I wanted to try my new skills of winning games on a grown up. I'd gotten so good, Connie wouldn't play with me anymore. I opened my closet. Heat blasted me, and I stumbled to the floor.

A tall man with mahogany skin the color of our coffee table towered above me. His suit, black and sleek, fit his body like a glove. He wore a cape reminding me of Zorro's. Long hair, wavy and pure white, hung to his waist, and his eyes were black, flecked with shards of rubies, oblong like a cat's. As he stared at me, the rubies blazed until they filled with fire.

He straddled the hole in large black boots so shiny I saw my reflection, but my face wasn't the only one looking back at me.

Daddy yelled from the kitchen. "Charlotte, did you fall in your closet?"

I forced myself from the floor. A chubby boy about my age stood next to the demon, clutching the handle of a small suitcase covered with sports decals. He held a basketball in his other arm with *Hades Undertows* written on top.

The boy had unruly black hair, the palest skin I had ever seen, and a lot of freckles. He had horns, too, and they stuck out of his head like the nubs of antlers on a young buck. He stepped into my room, dragging a navy blue tail that poked through his pants.

"See you later, Daddy."

The demon's answer cast an echo through my room. "Mind what I told you."

The boy smirked. "Oh, I'll remember everything."

The closet door slid in front of his father, and the temperature dropped at least ten degrees.

"Howdy, Sis. I'm Bo." He yanked the Chinese Checkers box out of my hands. "You don't mind if I take your turn playing with Daddy Walter, do you?"

French Twist

B o sauntered out of my room.

My hand trembled as I placed my palm on my closet door, pressed lightly, and slid it an inch. I peeked in. My shoes had fallen into the far corner, scattered around only one go-go boot.

Bo and Daddy's laughter filtered to my room. I knelt and ran my hand along the seamless floor. The other boot must have been swallowed back to Hell with Bo's father's disappearance.

Mommy opened my door. I grabbed a sneaker and pretended to straighten my shoes. She stepped behind me and pulled my Pilgrim dress off its hanger.

She watched me for a few seconds. "Thank you for straightening those. They always seem to be in a pile lately."

Mommy laid the dress on my bed and sat down. She patted the empty spot next to her. I joined her and leaned against her side. She'd put her hair up in a French twist and wore clip-on earrings covered in the same fabric as the dark blue dotted Swiss of her dress. The scent of cotton mixed with her perfumy deodorant. I touched her engagement ring and traced the small diamond with my index finger.

Would she say anything about Bo?

"We've got an hour before we have to go to the carnival. I'm so afraid your daddy is going to embarrass us tonight."

I fingered the diamond and moved it slightly back and forth. She'd wadded a tissue in her other hand.

"I don't know what else to do, Charlotte. I don't know how to support you and Connie on my own, not to mention facing the shame of being on welfare."

Being on welfare was the worst thing anybody could ever do. Even worse than being Catholic and getting a divorce.

Bo shouted from the kitchen. "I won! I won! Can we play another game, Daddy?"

A tear rolled down Mommy's face. "Charlotte, would you ask Daddy not to drink anymore today?"

"Do I have to?"

Mommy sniffled. "Of course, not. If I didn't feel so desperate, I wouldn't have said anything."

I didn't want to ask Daddy, but my prayer for Mommy hadn't been answered. I left her and walked into the hall. The walls expanded and contracted. A new door had appeared next to Connie's. Bo had dropped his suitcase in front of it. My stomach lurched the way it had on the teacup ride at Disneyland.

Why weren't my parents surprised they had a son living with them now? Why didn't Mommy say anything about the remodel of the house?

I swallowed. The hall stopped undulating. I stepped across to the suitcase and opened it. Bo had brought a few changes of underwear, a dozen or so pairs of socks, and a teddy bear with little horns matching his. I poked the teddy's tummy.

He frowned. "Watch it."

I slammed the suitcase shut and forced myself to find Daddy in the kitchen.

A picture taken at Sears when I was in kindergarten, and then tucked away in a photo album, now hung above the sofa, blown up to at least three sizes of the original. Connie and I wore matching yellow Easter dresses. Connie used to have her arm around a big plush pink bunny propped between us. Now she hugged Bo, a rotund little boy of about four in brown shorts and a yellow and white striped shirt. He held his tail like a blanket and stuck out his tongue. My sister and I wore lacy Easter hats. The little nubs of Bo's horns poked through his black hair.

I shuddered.

Bo and Daddy were engrossed in a new round at the table. I approached them almost on tiptoe. Daddy made a move and then took a long sip from his beer. I glanced up at the counter where a Jim Beam bottle sat next to a half full shot glass. He'd started on the watered-down whiskey.

Bo didn't bother to look up when he addressed me. "You got something to say, Charlotte?"

The bags below Daddy's eyes had the heavy look that always made me queasy. The clock ticked like a crazy person lived inside it. Tick. Tick. Ticktickticktick. Plenty of time for him to finish the bottle before we left.

My tongue grew thick in my mouth, but the tissue wadded in Mommy's hand and her tears had pushed me over the edge.

"Daddy,pleasedon'tdrinkanymoretoday."

"What did you say?"

Bo moved a marble. "Charlotte asked you not to drink anymore today."

Daddy's hand hit the board. Marbles flew across the room, clattered, bouncing everywhere and rolling under the refrigerator.

"Goddamn son of a bitch turning my daughter against me."

I never understood why Daddy called Mommy a *son* of a bitch. He reared out of his chair and cursed. Bo got up and opened the tall cabinet we used as a pantry and grabbed a box of Twinkies and some Ho Hos. He waddled out to the living room, his tail dragging marbles onto the carpet, turned on the TV, and switched channels until he got to Deputy Dawg. Then he climbed into the dark green recliner and tore open a package of Twinkies.

I loathed everything about Deputy Dawg. Deputy Dawg's doggy drawl made him sound half-tight himself. The cartoon was the stupidest one ever made in the whole world. Bo sure had mean instincts to turn it on in *my* house.

Daddy found Mommy. His yelling siphoned into the living room. "You're saying you're ashamed of me? You're ashamed of me?"

Mommy matched his volume. "No real man would get drunk every single day off, especially on a night so special for his daughter."

I bent down and picked marbles from the carpet.

"You're saying I'm not a man? You got your hair done up for that principal and for the goddamn real men tonight?"

Mommy rushed out of my room with Daddy at her heels. "Walter, it's a junior high Thanksgiving carnival, and Connie's principal is a woman. It's Connie's night, and you're ruining everything because you're a G.D. drunk."

In the kitchen, she nearly tripped on a marble as she made her way to the whiskey bottle. She unscrewed the lid and began pouring the drink into the sink. I stared at the next marble I planned to pick from the carpet. Daddy's shoes peeked from beneath his pant legs as he passed by me.

Mommy yelped in pain. "Let go of me."

I looked through my bangs. Daddy had grabbed Mommy's French Twist. Mommy dropped the bottle. An amber puddle spread across the floor encircling little islands of marbles that had scattered everywhere.

Half an hour later in the bathroom, I slipped my pilgrim's dress over the training bra I'd gotten for my birthday. I didn't like how my hair stuck out from the bottom of my cap. No Aqua Net for me. I poked the ends underneath and let my bangs show.

Mommy stood behind me. Her puffy eyes reflected from the mirror. Half of her French twist fell to the side of her head. "You look so cute. You'll be the cutest Pilgrim girl there."

I wanted to believe her. But I knew my status: lowly fourth grade sister. "I don't want to go without you, Mommy."

She nudged me out of the way to lean into the mirror and wipe some mascara smudged on her cheek. "I can't go like this. It's better this way. I can stay with Bo. He'd be bored at the carnival and get into mischief."

"Mom, about Bo? When did you first notice him?"

Her brow wrinkled for a moment, but then her lips curled into a sad smile. "In January, right after you were born. I was so surprised that I became pregnant again so fast."

Before we left home, Daddy hung his camera over his neck and strapped on his holster, saying he carried a badge and had every right to wear his gun any place he wanted to because he was a real man and a good cop. The fight with Mommy at least distracted him from drinking more. He needed two tries before he slid the key into the ignition, but he drove in straight lines to Connie's school.

In the gym, Connie stood behind a desk next to the cornucopia propped up on a couple of hay bales, selling tickets for the bean bag toss. Rhonda's brother, Jason, stood in front of four others in line. Jason had gotten horrible acne over the last six months or so. I studied his face with fascination as Daddy and I walked up.

Connie had her bossy look on. "No, you can't help, Jason. You're not on the student council. Just buy a ticket, will you?"

"But it's stupid for you to go back and forth to toss the bags back. Your vice-president didn't show up, did he?"

Connie frowned. "Oh, all right, but only until Jeff comes. He's bound to be here any minute."

Connie pestered me a lot to get a best friend with a cuter brother. But this is what she didn't know: the last time I'd gone over to Rhonda's house, we snuck into Jason's room. Rhonda opened his top dresser drawer and showed me a snapshot of Connie hidden there. I never said a word. Besides, seeing her face framed by white athletic socks creeped me out.

Daddy stumbled and then caught himself, leaning his hand on my shoulder.

Connie glared. "You were supposed to be here an hour ago. Where's Mom?"

I told her as much as I dared. "She had to stay home."

"But she's supposed to help Millie at the pie station. Was Bo being a pain?"

Give me a break. Connie had been at school when Bo emerged fully formed from my closet, and already she knew about him?

I did hope Bo behaved for Mommy. She'd had enough for one day. The next time Ezequiel turned up, boy, would I let him have it. He could have at least warned me a stupid demon brother was on his way.

Kids ran around. The scent of apple cider wafted from cups as people strolled by. Connie had done a good job getting this event together. If no show vice-president Jeff ever crossed my path, I'd bawl him out too.

Six kids now waited to throw bean bags into the horn. If they got one in, they'd get a goldfish. Seemed simple enough, but it looked like the original fifty fish were swimming in their bags. Daddy had said if Connie didn't get rid of them, we'd have them for supper on Sunday.

Very funny, ha-ha. But knowing Daddy, he might not be joking.

A boy in a Dwight Eisenhower Junior High black and gold football jersey tossed a bag that made a graceful arc toward the horn, and then, as if landing against a pane of glass, fell to the floor.

Jason tossed the bag back. "Bad luck, Freeman."

Freeman scowled. "You've rigged this."

Connie motioned for him to step aside. "Brady's turn now."

Connie's cap had slid cockeyed on her head. She lost the smile she left our house with, but a possible goldfish dinner in the makings might have had a lot to do with that.

Rhonda and Millie stood behind a table covered with pumpkin pies. At six thirty there would be a pie eating contest. I glanced at the clock above the bleachers. Ten minutes to go. Millie handed a boy named Richard an entry form. Connie said Richard had B.O., so I made a wide berth around him and joined Rhonda behind the table.

She lifted the lid to the cash box. "Look at the money we've made."

I counted the money quickly. "Fifteen dollars?"

Her blue eyes got bigger. "And thirty-eight cents."

Millie finished with Richard and came over to us. "Charlotte, you look adorable. Is June here?"

"She doesn't feel good.

Millie looked at Daddy as he took the cap off of his camera in front of the cornucopia. "I am sorry to hear she's sick."

When Rhonda and I were little, before Millie got divorced and started working, Mommy and she used to have coffee together at least once a week in our kitchen. The two of us played together on the floor while our mothers talked about our fathers and spelled out dirty words. One of them formed on Millie's lip.

Daddy's voice carried from where he stood. "Stand by the horn, Connie."

He took forever to focus the camera. Connie looked like one unhappy Pilgrim. Finally, Daddy took the picture and used his loud policeman voice. "Hey, everyone, this is my beautiful daughter, Connie Jackson, the best seventh grade president this damn school ever had."

Everyone in the gym froze. A nervous spatter of applause broke out.

Connie stepped close to him. "Daddy, stop."

Daddy's volume dipped a little. "Get back there and smile this time."

He lifted the camera again, and his coat fell open.

As the flash flickered, Jason yelled, "Mr. Jackson's got a gun!"

The gym grew quiet like we were all going to say a prayer, but then a gray-haired woman in black pumps rushed over to Daddy, her shoes click-clacking on the shiny floor.

"What's going on?"

Daddy pulled his badge out of his pocket. "Sergeant Walter Jackson, LVPD. My daughter is the seventh grade president."

Even in her heels, the woman didn't come up to Daddy's chin, but she stood close enough so she had to have smelled his breath. "I'm Mrs. Schulz, the principal. I'm going to have to ask you to leave, Mr. Jackson."

Daddy didn't like anyone telling him what to do. He aimed his camera again and snapped another picture.

"Mr. Jackson—"

"Connie, Charlotte, we're leaving."

Mrs. Shultz didn't flinch. "I can't let the girls go with you. I'll find someone to take them home. I'll call a taxi for you."

Disgust filled Daddy's face. "The hell you will."

He strode out of the gym while the whole junior high watched.

A few moments later Millie announced, "Time for the contest," and the gym buzzed again. Jason tossed Freeman another bean bag. Freeman threw it, but once again the bag arced through the air until it fell to the floor as though it hit a wall.

Connie became a statue, no tears, but with a beet red face, and I felt like I'd turned inside out.

❧❧❧

We were two lost Pilgrim sisters. Millie drove us home after the carnival ended. No one had won a fish. In the back of the station wagon, Connie and Jason held the tank with the goldfish. Rhonda and I were latched into seatbelts in the middle of the car. Millie was the only grown up I knew who insisted on using them, and it felt scary to have a belt around my lap.

No light came from the house except for a bluish glow from the TV shining through the drapes. Mom had left the door unlocked, which *never* happened. We found Bo in the recliner with Twinkie and Ho Ho wrappers scattered around the chair.

He farted. "Mommy went to bed."

I walked over and kicked the footrest down. "Help Connie and Jason with the tank."

A commercial sang *See the U.S.A. in your Chevrolet,* as the three of them carried the tank to the kitchen table. Millie disappeared down the hall to check on Mommy.

Bo put his hand in, grabbed one of the goldfish, and kissed it. "Lucky fishy." He dropped it back in the water. "Daddy's not going to like seeing these back here. We'd better do something."

I switched on the kitchen light. "Like what?"

A huge grin broke above Bo's double chin. "Let's flush them."

Rhonda spread her arms across the threshold between the kitchen and the living room. "I'm not letting you kill the fish."

Mommy's crying echoed from her bedroom.

Bo cocked his head. "I won't let you be my girlfriend, Rhonda, if you stop us."

The boys picked up the tank. To my amazement, Rhonda stepped away and let them pass. Water and fish sloshed from side to side as they hauled it into the bathroom.

Rhonda stood at the bathroom door with a blank look on her face. I shoved past her, moved around the boys, opened the cupboard under the sink, and grabbed the little bowl stashed there. Connie and I had tried having goldfish once before. After our grief from finding them belly up one morning, Daddy laid down the law about pets. Never again.

The boys lifted the tank and fish poured into the toilet. I put the fishbowl under the stream and managed to catch one.

Bo made a kissy sound. "Lucky fishy, Goldie."

Jason flushed the toilet, and both he and Bo laughed hysterically. Connie yelled for Mommy, and she and Millie came running.

I leaned over the sink and turned on the faucet to fill Goldie's new home. "The boys flushed all of the fish except for this one."

Bo put his hands up like he was about to be arrested. "Jason's the one who thought of it. I tried to stop him, honestly."

Jason's smile ripped from his face. "He's lying."

Millie yanked Jason into the hall by the collar of his tee shirt. "Into the car now. I'll check in on you tomorrow, June."

Connie disappeared into her room. I took Goldie to the safety of mine and found Ezequiel sitting cross-legged on my bed. How dare he show up at this moment!

I put Goldie on my nightstand and then turned on him. "Who's the scary guy in my closet? And who's this little creep of a brother I suddenly got?"

Ezequiel uncrossed his legs and let them hang. "I'm doing the best I can, Cupcake."

"Don't you ever call me Cupcake again. I am not a cupcake."

I made a fist and tried to punch him, but he caught my arm. "Calm down, will you?"

I swung my other arm and landed a blow on his shoulder.

"Ouch." Ezequiel stood up, rubbing it. "Look, this is how it is. That guy's name is Abraxas and he's my boss. He ordered me to turn you to our side if I'm going to keep visiting."

I'd planned on walloping him again, but my arms dropped to my side.

Ezequiel bent down to eye level with me. "I refused. Bo's the consequence. They sent him to stir things up. His real name is Behemoth. Abraxas, by the way, is the one who really runs the show in Hell. Satan is old and tired and pretty much a wimp these days."

A shiver ran through me. "Is something bad going to happen to me?"

Ezequiel glanced at my window. "Not if I can help it."

The headlights of Daddy's car spanned through my drapes and across my window. A minute later, the car pulled into the garage. Pins and needles. The door opened in the kitchen. Silence. And then Mommy's muffled voice.

I'd shut my bedroom door securely, but it swung open as though the house wanted me in on the action.

"What were you thinking, abandoning those girls?"

Daddy's words blurred together. "I didn't abandon them. The girls weren't at school."

"For God's sake, Walter, the carnival ended two hours ago."

Goldie swam placidly in her little bowl. I needed to get a castle for her and maybe some of those magic rocks that grew overnight.

Connie's voice reverberated now. She must have joined my parents. "I'm never going back to school again."

"Get off my back, the two of you."

I jumped up. Ezequiel grabbed my arm. "Charlotte, don't go out there."

"What if he hurts her?"

I didn't know if I meant Mommy or Connie. I pulled from Ezequiel's grasp and rushed to the kitchen. Mommy must have hit Daddy because his glasses were on the floor. He shoved her against the sink with Connie wedged between them.

Bo perched on the counter a few feet away lazily peeling a banana and winked at me. I wanted to squish it in his face. He flicked his tail. "Go on, I dare you."

He stuck out his tongue, long and purple like a Chow Chow's.

Ezequiel picked me up. "I'm getting you out of here."

He carried me back to my room and into the closet. The floor opened, and heat engulfed us. We fell for a long time. I buried my face into his chest, my nose squished into his jacket. When we landed, I dropped from his arms and threw up. I spit out the vomit remaining in my mouth.

"May I have a glass of water?"

"No can do, but I have some warm Coke in my filing room. You'd better not look at anything until we get there."

"No can do, Ezequiel."

I wanted to see the details. I mean, I *was* in Hell.

We appeared to be in a huge cave. Crates marked "martini glasses" and "poker chips" and a long thin box with "Contractual Agreements" printed on it were stacked on a platform. A large sign hung next to the crates. Someone had taken a marker and written "The devil is in the details" above my address in a cursive that could only be admired.

"Do you think it will help"— I pointed upward—"if we prayed to the Virgin right now?"

Ezequiel's face blanched. "Not a good idea, Charlotte. The walls have ears. Let's go."

We left the big room and entered a narrow passageway that made me think of the little tunnels of the ant farm in Mr. Ortega's class. Ezequiel had to be joking, right? Then I noticed tiny mouse size ears surrounding us and closed eyelids quivering like they were dreaming.

We passed door after door with metal numbers on them like at a motel and then veered to the right. Ezequiel stopped, pulling a skeleton key from his pocket to open Room 777.

I'd had a long day. I wanted to dream like the eyes on the wall, but seeing Ezequiel's number perked me up.

"Hey, you've got a lucky address.

Demon Juice

The door to Room 777 opened with a squeak that set my teeth on edge. I followed Ezequiel in my Pilgrim dress and the pair of white Keds I'd slipped on my feet before Daddy took me to the carnival. My underarms grew moist beneath the long sleeves. Too bad the Pilgrims hadn't worn shorts on the first Thanksgiving.

We walked into an annex Ezequiel lived in—was dead in—not much bigger than my bedroom. A thing I'd never seen the likes of, halfway between a TV and a typewriter, with another strange contraption about the size of a breadbox and connecting to it with wires, rested on top of a desk made of bleached wood.

A lime green plastic chair had been shoved under the table, not too different from the one Mr. Ortega used for the reading groups in the back of my classroom. A white refrigerator rested against the wall next to the door with its power cord curled on the floor like a thin black snake. I didn't see an outlet.

The far side of the annex opened to a warehouse of sorts. Curious, I peeked in. It stretched out so far that eternity might have had room to park inside. Row after row of gray-metal cabinets stacked like library shelves went on forever.

On the first row, directly across from where I stood, a sign labeled Aa-Ab stuck out on top like a little flag. The next row had one that said Aba-Abc.

A cart reminding me of ones I'd seen at the Ponderosa Saloon in Virginia City, which had been used for silver ore, rested on a track that disappeared into the vast distance. This one, though, had a bench seat in the front like a ride at Disneyland. In the back, a bin was completely filled with papers.

I turned around and gave Ezequiel's quarters a quick evaluation. "Where do you sleep?"

He stretched his arms out. "In my lovely home? No sleep in Hell. No food. No movies. No radio. There's TV in some rooms, but they only show the news. I'll get the Coke."

As he walked to the fridge, I noticed the absence of one important thing. "No bathroom?"

He put his hand on the fridge's handle but didn't open it. "You don't have to go, do you?"

I shook my head, so he took out a Coke. He walked to the table and snapped off the lid with a bottle opener attached to the side of the desk.

"What about your air conditioning? You didn't get it?"

"Yeah, I did, but as soon as I stop working, it turns off."

He handed me my drink. I took a sip, washing the nastiness from my mouth with the nastiness of Coke the temperature of bath water. "This is awful."

"You get used to it. Look, Charlotte, I showed up tonight because the computer said a ninety-eight percent chance a major blow out would happen between your parents. My guess is things are getting pretty dismal right about now."

"The what?"

He pointed to the machine on his desk. "We're trying out prototypes."

I had no idea what "prototype" meant, but I knew the math and didn't need my fingers. 100 minus 98. "What about the other two percent?"

"Free will. Your mother had the choice to let you and Connie go home with Millie. She could have left your dad tonight too."

Sweat streamed down my back. I took a big swig, made a face, and set the bottle next to the computer. "You're wrong, Ezequiel. Mommy would never leave Daddy. I'm 100 percent sure she wouldn't."

"Whatever you want to believe." Ezequiel swept an arm toward the files. "Want to see the operation?"

We walked into the big room. Mommy and Daddy took Connie and me to Death Valley once in August to see how hot it would be. We stopped at a place called Badwater, the lowest location in North America. The room had the same ambiance.

Ezequiel leaned against the cart. "My job is to file the records of what happens in everyone's day. Once I put them in folders the papers disappear, so I have no idea why I have to do it."

I didn't believe him. "Everyone's on Earth? That's impossible."

"You think? Actually, there's about a million of us grunts who do this work. Somehow by the end of my shift, the cart is empty. Don't ask me how it works."

Ezequiel grabbed a few papers. "Bo can only hurt you if you let him."

I didn't believe him for a second. "He's horrible."

"You're right, but I'm going to let you in on the first lesson they teach us at school down here. When people think they're powerless, it's one of the ways demons come to Earth, but hardly anyone has ever figured this out, especially not on their own. And the most common way people get entrapped is by thinking someone else has the power to make them unhappy."

Ezequiel shook his head and looked quickly at the paper on top. "Like this poor soul. Aaaqil Aab. His file happens to be the very first one. Hasn't talked to his brother in thirty years for getting the bulk of the family's inheritance. He'd rather stew in old stale anger. Pure demon juice."

I took another sip of Coke and made a face. "This tastes like demon juice."

Ezequiel tossed the papers back into the cart. "I should get back to work. You want to help?"

"Sure."

"You want to see Paul McCartney's day? I can do a special print out."

I never had said a word about my crush on Paul to Ezequiel. I felt exposed. On his first visit, Ezequiel said he knew everything about me. So, did he know I kissed Paul's picture in *Tiger Beat*? Or about my daydream about the double decker bus ride? The room grew so hot I felt I couldn't breathe.

But I DID want the lowdown on Paul. "Sure."

I followed Ezequiel back to the computer. "I'm not sure why we have to do the damn filing by hand when the info is already on the LavaNet. The extra work is absurd, but my boss doesn't want to give up the old ways. It's part of the torture, I think."

He leaned across the chair, not bothering to sit down, and began to type on the typewriter part. In a few seconds, the machine next to it whirred and a printed paper came out the top.

The air conditioner turned on. I bathed in the cool air until Ezequiel handed me Paul's paper.

I read aloud. "Paul McCartney, Born June 18, 1942. He had tea and scones for breakfast. What are scones?"

"Beats me."

"Then he took his dog for a walk."

Paul was having a pretty boring day, but I would have loved to show the paper to Rhonda. "Can I take this home with me?"

Ezequiel's face hardened. He'd never looked stern before, and his expression scared me. "Never take anything from Hell other than matches." I tried to hand the paper back, but he shook his head. "You can file it for me."

"Can I take a peek at Rhonda's day?"

Ezequiel's hands flew across the computer. Out popped another paper.

I skimmed the note. She'd helped Millie make pies for the festival. She ate a grilled cheese sandwich for lunch. Jason teased her, and she tattled on him.

But, unlike Paul's paper, a commentary had been added in the same beautiful handwriting as on the note on the box of contracts.

Overweight, but on a diet even at her young age. Highly sensitive to criticism. How can we undermine this? Has written in her diary Charlotte Johnson, her best friend, is bossy.

Hey, not fair! With a sister like Connie, I knew all about being bossed around. How dare Rhonda think I was like that. Besides, she let Bo flush the goldfish. She was an accomplice in murder.

Maybe she needed someone to set her straight, and maybe I was the person for the job. Coke, mixed with bile, rose from my stomach and burned my throat. Yep, pure demon juice.

We got into the cart. I clutched Paul and Rhonda's papers to my chest and let the cool air caress my face as we glided next to the cabinets. We whizzed by the "Jacl-Jack" section. Everyone in my family must have had their file folder tucked in among many hundreds of thousand somewhere way back in the corridor.

Wait! Mommy's maiden name was Marshall. Did her file get moved after she married Daddy? I wanted to ask Ezequiel, but he stared straight ahead. He had a job to do.

The cart passed by what seemed like a thousand more aisles, and then he pushed a red button. A puff exited from the back of the cart, and it slowed with what sounded like brakes made of pure air.

We were at the McCAs. There must be a lot of people whose names started with those letters because they had two rows all their own.

Work Ezequiel didn't have as much fun as the Ezequiel who came to visit to play games and sing songs. "Do you understand alphabetical order?"

I put my hands on my hips. "Ezequiel, please. Do I look like a second grader?"

Probably not my best argument. A few second graders had more than an inch on me.

"Okay, smarty pants." He pointed down the narrow aisles between the cabinet's walls. "Paul McCartney's file is about a quarter mile down, on the left near the bottom. Rhonda's, about another half mile on the right. It's fairly high up."

He wanted me to walk down there by myself in the dark?

"Is there scary stuff?"

"The only scary things are the countless stories of people's miserable lives. Hey, you'll be fine."

Ezequiel reached over my head and switched on a light beneath the sign. I hadn't noticed the switch before or the red button beneath it. Drawers stacked from floor to ceiling must have stretched from here to the other end of Hell.

"This will give you something to do while I find homes for the rest of these." He jabbed his thumb toward the car. "And this is the best part, better than even riding in the cart."

Ezequiel pushed the button and the part of the ceiling opened about a foot wide. A ladder unfolded like a string of paper dolls. He maneuvered the ladder so it connected to a rail on the ceiling running in the middle of the corridor.

"Hop on and hold tight. Say Paul's full name, and you'll be taken to his drawer. You can climb up or down to reach it, whatever you need to do. Be sure you put the paper in the file marked with his birthday, because about fifteen thousand Paul McCartneys are currently alive."

Finding the correct place sounded a lot harder than the ABC order worksheets Mr. Ortega mimeographed for us. I tucked Paul's and Rhonda's papers in a pocket, climbed up three steps, and grabbed the bars on either side.

"I'll meet you back here in about an hour. Say 'Exit' when you want to return." He placed his hand over my left one. "You'll do fine, Charlotte."

I squeezed until my fingers hurt. "Paul McCartney."

The ladder vibrated as it gained speed. My dress billowed behind me, and the same sweet fresh air as on our ride in the cart cooled my face. Nothing frightening happened, but there sure wasn't a view. I flew through a valley of towering cabinets for a minute or two and then the ladder slowed to a gentle stop.

The drawer next to me was labeled *McCartney, Pauli-Payge*. I said the ABCs to myself. Okay, I could do this. I stepped up a rung.

McCartney Pamela-Paul.

Got it! The ladder rotated to let me pull open the drawer. Paul, Paul, Paul, Paul, Paul. So many of them! But they were organized by months with birth dates after the names, starting with January 2, 1895. It only took a moment to find the two Paul McCartneys born in June, one on June 12, 1964. Behind baby Paul, my file lay at my fingertips. Luck was with me that my Paul had been born in the only unpopular month.

Maybe I'd find out something cool, like the Beatles' next album, or some gossip about Jane Asher, his girlfriend. My fingers wiggled in excitement. I slipped them into the file.

Nothing there.

"Hmph."

I took Paul's paper from my pocket and tried to smooth the creases. I placed it inside the folder and watched it vanish like a snow cone dropped on a sidewalk in July. The drawer silently shut. The ladder rotated back and waited for the next direction.

"Rhonda McCauley."

The ladder sped away. I passed Mcthises and Mcthats until it stopped. Okay, Rhonda's now. Right side. Fairly high up. I climbed higher and found the drawer.

Holy moley! How many Rhonda McCauleys lived on Planet Earth? I had to stretch to get to the ones born in May.

Found it! Rhonda Marie McCauley May 29, 1956.

Ezequiel's voice echoed down the aisle. "How are you doing?"

An hour had already passed?

"Almost done."

I held open Rhonda's file, but my fingers didn't want to let go of her paper. How would one day of a nine-year-old girl's life be missed, especially since it would vanish in plain sight once I dropped it into the file? I'd show what the paper said to Rhonda to prove I'd gone to Hell and give her a piece of my mind about her attitude.

I put the paper into my back pocket. The drawer snapped shut with a little more energy than Paul's.

I said the magic word. "Exit."

The ladder spun around and off I went.

Ezequiel sat in front of a completely empty cart. He gave me a big smile. "Ready to finish your bottle of Coke?"

A craving to have more filled me, even though my stomach already burned in anticipation of how the drink would hit it. By the time Ezequiel parked the cart, my mouth watered for a taste of the warm liquid.

In his annex, Ezequiel pulled out a Coke for himself and popped the lid open. I picked up my bottle from where I left it, and we clicked them together.

The air conditioning turned off, and the handle to his door began to turn.

Ezequiel's face blanched. "What's he doing here at this hour?"

"Who?"

Ezequiel filled me in quickly. "A messenger goon called Kimaris. He runs errands and finds lost items. He's pretty useless other than being a grunt. He's been helping me take the casino equipment up to Earth."

With that lovely piece of information, I watched the door swing open. I covered my ears to protect them from the nails on a chalkboard screech.

Kimaris's bulk filled the doorway. He slid into the room like a slug. *Squish. Squish.* I didn't dare look at his face, so I stared at his webbed hands holding my lost go-go boot.

"Knews I'd finds her here. I watched the two of yous land by the portal."

He tossed the boot at me. It landed on my chest with a thud. I wrapped my arms around it and really wanted to potty.

Ezequiel's halo burned brighter. He winced.

Kimaris laughed. "Angel Boy gots a headache. The boss wants to see us. I suggests this little girl you're diddling goes back to her homey-home."

Ezequiel turned beat red, even his hands became the color of blood. His horns shot out the sparkly light I'd grown to love, but his face contorted like he held himself from throttling Mr. Goon. "Charlotte is only nine, Kamiris. She's a little girl."

Kimaris snorted. "She ain't gonna stay little much longer." He slurped out.

Ezequiel took a pocket watch from inside his jacket. His skin had faded to the color of a dead rose. "It's 2:45 in Las Vegas. I'm sure things have quieted down at your house, Cupcake."

I held back from saying, "I'm not a cupcake."

He reached into the other side of his jacket and pulled out a matchbook. "Always bring it when you come here. When you light a match, it will take you home. Do you understand?"

"I think so." But where could I hide them so Mommy wouldn't find them?

The fireworks from his horns had stopped. They'd faded to pale pink.

"Okay." Ezequiel glanced toward the door. "You need to go home."

"But we're not at the portal."

"Can't be helped. It'll be a longer trip, but you'll get there."

I pulled a match from the book, but stopped before I struck it. I'd wedged my boot under my arm. I looked at it and then back at Ezequiel. "Should I take this?"

Ezequiel nodded. "You weren't the one who took the boot from here."

I pulled a match from the book. I had to scratch it three times before it would light, but it finally sizzled and then a snap, crackle, pop like Rice Krispies in my cereal bowl surrounded me.

Everything grew dark. Despite Ezequiel's earlier warning, I started praying. *JesusMaryGod, help me help me help me.*

I left Hell proper. The earth squeezed me. I smelled dirt but none of it got in my nose. I could at least breathe. I flew up through my closet floor which sealed itself shut before I made an amazingly gentle landing. Prayer answered.

I arranged my shoes in darkness: my saddle oxfords, my patent leather Mary Janes, my flip-flops, my sneakers. I put the recovered go-go boot next to the other one in the middle.

I crawled to my nightstand and turned on the light.

Goldie still swam in circles.

"Don't you ever sleep? Are you hungry?"

Connie had left fish food next to the kitchen sink. I felt along the dark hallway, the muted glow of the nightlight in the kitchen guiding me. I grabbed the container.

"Charlotte?"

Daddy sat in one of the dinette chairs, his arms on his thighs as though he had been holding his head in his hands. "I won't drink again. I promise."

I held the fish food close to my heart. I walked to him and kissed the top of his head.

Spawn of Satan

I hadn't sucked my thumb since kindergarten, but I woke up with it in my mouth. I'd fallen asleep in my Pilgrim dress. The bedspread and sheets had been smoothed around me, but I didn't remember being tucked in.

I curled into a ball, not wanting to admit a new day had arrived. I wished I'd slept for hours more and not remember Connie squished between my parents as they battled in the kitchen. I curled tighter as I relived falling to Hell and being squeezed by the Earth on the way back.

The doorbell rang.

"Captain Hartson, please come in."

Mommy didn't sound pleased. Daddy's boss showing up couldn't be a good thing.

The recliner squeaked. Daddy must have been sitting in it.

The captain's voice boomed, even though I don't think he intended it to. That was just the way he talked. "Don't get up, Walt."

I eased myself out of bed and peeked out.

Mommy caught me staring. "Why are you in your costume? Go change and stay in your room."

I took a step back but kept the door open a crack.

Mommy took on a very polite tone. "Would you like some coffee, Captain Hartman?"

"No, thank you."

"Won't you have a seat?"

"I don't think so."

A few seconds passed. In my mind's eye, Mommy pulled out a tissue from a pocket and twisted it into a tight roll.

The captain's deep voice rolled down the hall. "Walt, I guess I might as well say this straight. I got a call from Mrs. Schultz about last night."

Did Daddy make fists with his hands? No, not in front of his boss. I pictured him a thousand feet away from Captain Hartson, like a magnet had pulled him into a lonely corner of a strange house.

His voice did sound far away. "I had ever right—"

The captain interrupted. "You had no right to come to an event drunk and wearing your gun. You're suspended for two weeks. With pay. This time. But if you—"

"I'll work a desk for as long as you say, Mike." I imagine Daddy floating across the long room, coming closer. "I promise, no drinking."

Connie stood in her doorway, and we stared across at each other. I wished I had tears streaming down my face the way she did, but other than sensing Mommy's embarrassment I was numb. That hurt enough.

"Walt, come to my office first thing on the 9th. I'll see myself out."

I took a tentative step forward. Connie took one too. Mommy and the captain stood at the end of the hall. He opened the door and sunlight streamed in, illuminating dust particles that danced around their bodies.

"Captain Hartman, I appreciate your kindness."

"Take care of yourself, Mrs. Jackson."

He bowed his head ever so slightly and left.

Connie closed her door as though it were made of gauze.

By then, Daddy had crossed the living room. "What the hell was that about?" He grabbed Mommy's shoulders. "What's going on between the two of you?"

She tried to pull away. "What in the world would make you think something is happening between me and that man?"

Daddy's face turned crimson. "I goddamn know what I just saw."

Mom turned her head. "Charlotte, out of that dress. Get back to your room."

Bo toddled from his room, transformed into the age of the little demon in the Easter picture. His pjs were decorated with red fighter jets blazing across a white background. He clutched his demon teddy who I swear gave me a dirty look.

"Daddy sad?"

Mom yanked herself from Daddy's grasp, ignoring both Bo and me as she rushed past the two of us and disappeared into her bedroom.

Bo waddled to Daddy and took his hand. Daddy muttered something in a nasty tone I couldn't make out about Mommy, but he picked up my new brother who wrapped his arms and legs around him and snuggled against his neck.

⟫⟫⟫ ⟪⟪⟪

Connie sulked in her room while I drew pictures of Hell in mine, coloring the file cabinets and the bin of papers yellow and pink. Their severe gray was the most depressing thing I'd found the night before. I let the color turquoise flood my mind and clicked my pen to draw the walls and decorated them with bright purple flowers blooming between the ears and the sleeping eyes.

I remembered I'd dropped the matchbook in the closet next to my boots. I slipped it into the cover of my Herman's Hermits album. Connie called me a dork for liking them, so she'd never borrow it. As long as I put the record away, Mommy would have no reason to touch it.

I'd wadded Rhonda's paper into the back pockets of the pants I'd changed into. It immediately seared my butt.

Eventually, I became hungry enough to risk going out to the kitchen. I got a big bowl of Cap'n Crunch and then wandered into the living room. Daddy and Bo were watching Billy Graham preaching at the Astrodome.

So, this was Daddy's favorite joke:

A guy from Arkansas traveled to Texas. He went to a restaurant and ordered a steak. When the waitress brought it, he exclaimed about its enormous size.

"Everything's big in Texas," the waitress said.

He then ordered a beer. It came in a huge glass.

The waitress told him, "Everything's big in Texas."

Then the guy needed to go to the bathroom. The waitress told him to step out the back door to find the toilet. He followed her directions. He walked out and found a swimming pool.

"Well," the guy said, "everything *is* big in Texas."

Daddy told this joke a million times. He considered it funnier than "What did the big chimney say to the little chimney?" which was my personal favorite.

While Billy preached, the camera panned over the crowd of what might have been 60,000 people. Everything *was* big in Texas. Billy filled the screen as he spoke of God from the bottom of his heart. Close-ups of devout faces appeared. A grandmotherly woman nodded her head. A young man, so serious he scared me, held a Bible to his heart. In succession, several homespun types cried, wiped tears with hankies, or blew their noses.

Daddy had stubble on his face and now held a cup of black coffee. Bo sat beside him, grasping a Frito's bag. Crumbs covered his cheeks. He patted the recliner seat with his tail. In daylight, the skin looked slimy.

"Repent and accept the Lord Jesus," Billy entreated, "or face eternity in Hell."

Bo popped a Frito in his mouth and gave me a once over. "Hell bad place, Charlotte?"

I could barely swallow. Did Bo know where I'd been? Did he know Rhonda's paper now burned my butt?

Daddy gave me hope, though. Eleven in the morning on a day off, and no beer was in sight. Maybe Captain Hartman's visit shook him up, despite Daddy's crazy jealousy. A sliver of hope rose inside me, like the sun peaking over the horizon on a cold, cold morning.

Bo rubbed his head against Daddy's arm like a cat demanding to be petted. His horns bent back and almost disappeared in his thick hair. Daddy put his arm around him. With his other hand, he picked up the phone to dial the number on the TV.

"Yes, I need someone to pray with me."

Smoke trickled out of Bo's exposed ear. His tail twitched. He slid off of Daddy's lap and toddled to the set, his tail dragging a line of Fritos across the carpet. He switched channels.

A sultry voice glided from the TV.

The Grand Opening of Burning Sands Casino.

The only place to be this New Year's Eve.

Fountains of fire spouted in front of a palace with a facade of what looked like white marble. The view panned in closer toward a red gemlike portico leading to huge crystalline doors. Above them, etched in shining gold were the words BURNING SANDS WELCOMES YOU in eight-foot high handwriting that I'd been coming upon far too often.

Pictures of smiling people at slot machines and young women dancing in feathers barely covering their private places blended into one another.

Come try your luck at Burning Sands

You'll never want to leave

Our tables are hot, our drinks sublime

You'll want to stay and bet your life

Burning Sands Casino

The only place to be

This coming New Year's Eve

Rhonda's paper smoldered in my pocket. I didn't want to be angry anymore. I rushed outside to the patio, tore the paper into shreds and threw them in the trash can.

Bo joined me as I closed the lid. He'd turned into an eight-year-old again.

"What did you throw away?"

"None of your business. Go back to Daddy and get some religion."

More smoke shot out Bo's ears. "I'm going to see Jason. Want to come?"

"His family won't be back from Mass yet. It's Sunday, and they always go to Denny's afterwards."

Bo shook his head in mock horror. "Oh, goodness, it's Sunday. And Jason would never refuse to go to church, would he?"

He sauntered past me and out the backyard gate. My rear heated up again. I reached in the pocket and felt Rhonda's paper, blazing to my touch.

By the early evening, Daddy started throwing up. Mommy left her bedroom to put some TV dinners in the oven for Connie and me and to fill an ice pack for Daddy's head.

I tested reality. "What about Bo's dinner?"

Mommy didn't answer. Even when Millie called to see if Jason had come over, Mommy only said, "Haven't seen him today," and then started to whisper to Millie about Daddy retching in the bathroom.

I turned to look at the Christmas picture. Only the barest outline of Bo remained, his form like one of those dot-to-dot worksheets. I stepped into the hallway and blinked as it expanded and retracted. The portion that held Bo's room faded.

The hall shifted back and forth. I held on to the wall and staggered toward Connie's room. She sat on the side of her bed as though the smell of the aluminum wrapped food in the oven had brought her back from the dead. Dark circles under her eyes looked like smudges of charcoal. Even though I was afraid she'd bite my head off, I stepped inside.

Connie glared at me. "I can't go to school tomorrow. Everyone will be talking behind my back."

A lot of kids from my school had brothers and sisters at Dwight Eisenhower, some of the kids had even been at the carnival. The next day wasn't going to be different for me.

My parent's bedroom was at the back of the house on Connie's side. The sink's faucet turned on and a low groan penetrated the wall.

I stuck my head out Connie's door. "Mommy, I think Daddy might be dying."

"He thinks he needs a drink. Ignore him." She went back to her conversation with Millie.

The hallway expanded and shrank. I said a prayer for Daddy. I promised to be nice to Connie and to Rhonda and to everyone on Earth including Jason, if absolutely necessary. I promised to talk my family into going to church if this would free us of Bo and the rest of the demonic hosts.

I ran into my bathroom and once again shredded Rhonda's day, flushing the pieces down the toilet where they went to meet the goldfish. Looking down the hall, other than hearing Daddy puke, things finally appeared normal.

Later that night, Daddy's stomach had settled, He sounded like a grizzly bear snoring in the back of the house. As usual, Mommy ordered me to bed halfway through Ed Sullivan. My cheek burned as it touched my pillow. I reached underneath and found Rhonda's paper again freshly type, pressed flat without a crease.

⟫⟫⟩ ⟨⟨⟨⟪

The next morning, Connie walked out of the house as though she were going to her own execution. Bo hadn't come home.

I lingered a while longer. I didn't have any pockets in my dress, so I put my note in my Herman's Hermit album, tucking it in with the matchbook.

By the time I got to the bus stop, Jason sat next to Connie on the bench, his face a mirror of her own depression. To my dismay, Bo and Rhonda crowded with them. The four of them barely fit. Bo opened the *F Troop* lunchbox on his lap and handed Rhonda a Hostess Cupcake. She shoved almost half of it in her mouth.

I ran up with clenched fists ready to deck him. "You leave Rhonda alone."

Bo mashed the cupcake's twin between his teeth, sharing Rhonda's chipmunk look, wide-eyed and fat cheeked. Chocolate frosting leaked out the sides of both of their mouths.

Rhonda clearly needed my advice.

"If you keep eating cupcakes at this time of the morning, you're going to be a lot more than pleasantly plump."

I squished my eyebrows together to show her how serious I was.

Rhonda stopped mid-chew. The junior high bus pulled up. Connie bent her head so low, her hair covered her entire face. Jason took her arm and led her to the door.

Bo pulled out another cupcake package from his lunch box. "Thanks for nothing, Jason."

The door closed with a whoosh. Jason yanked down his window and stuck his head outside. "Leave my sister alone."

The bus drove away.

My head whipped back to Bo and Rhonda. "Why is he so upset?"

Bo talked through the cupcake in his mouth. "Unfortunately, Jason has a heart after all."

Rhonda swallowed enough to speak. "Mom grounded Jason."

"Like that's new?"

Our bus arrived. Rhonda stood, clasping her *I Dream of Jeanie* lunchbox. "This time Jason asked her to do it."

Bo shrugged innocently enough, but narrowed his eyes in vexation. "He wouldn't pull the trick on Connie that I needed him to."

Rhonda bit into the new cupcake Bo offered. "Jason's in love with Connie. And Bo's in love with me, so keep your opinions to yourself, Charlotte, about what I choose to eat."

The other kids climbed aboard the bus. Mr. Tommy, the old gray-haired driver, frowned under his cap and crossed his arms. Before he said anything about us getting a move on, I pulled myself up the steps.

Rhonda sat beside me on the hard green seat on the right side of the second row like she did every day. Bo made a beeline to the back.

She licked her fingers one by one. "I talked Bo out of hurting Connie's feelings. He planned on teasing her this morning about your dad. But when I said I'd be disappointed in him, he promised he wouldn't."

We went over a bump, and a loud fart rebounded through the bus. The boys in the far back cheered.

"Rhonda, you don't know what Bo is."

"Oh, yes, I do."

She turned in her seat and waved at him. Bo sat on his haunches on the bench. His tail turned to a shade of mauve. He fashioned it into a heart shape as he mouthed I LOVE YOU.

Even though Rhonda said she didn't want to hear my opinions, I offered one anyway. "Disgusting!"

"I think he's cute. Charlotte, I know he's the spawn of Satan, but he doesn't care what I eat. He accepts me for who I am."

Her penetrating stare dared me to say anything about the last bite of the second cupcake resting between her right thumb and forefinger.

She knew Bo's history?

"What's a spawn?"

"I have no idea, but Bo says all demons are spawns of Satan. Metaphorically speaking."

"Huh?"

Rhonda didn't explain. "Charlotte, I'm sorry I thought you were lying when you mentioned Ezequiel. But now we both have boyfriends."

My lunch pail with The Beatles, of course, grew warm in my lap. "He told you about Ezequiel?"

She nodded.

"Ezequiel's not my boyfriend, Rhonda, and Bo isn't anything like him. He's evil. Ezequiel is—" I needed a moment to consider my words. "He took a wrong turn."

"Bo's not evil either." Rhonda turned her face to the window. "You don't always know everything."

Ringo's drum set burned through my dress. I opened my lunch box. The paper rested on top of my peanut butter and jelly sandwich with the same branding iron seal that had embossed Ezequiel's diploma.

Mr. Teddy parked the bus. I clicked the pail shut, grabbed the handle tight, even though the heat made my fingers smart, and left my friend sitting there.

On the playground, Bo followed me to the Lucky 13s. Several third graders who'd been part of the Safe 11s classroom lined up with us.

What? A combo class now?

When we got inside, Mr. Olivera and the kids acted like Bo and the other third graders had always been part of our room. I studied the class photo Mr. Olivera pinned on the wall by the door, and, sure enough, Bo stood behind me with two fingers behind my head.

We were assigned a boring ditto where we had to find the right place to put the accent on our vocabulary words and then read a story about a million pages long. After that, we had a lesson on long division.

Everyone had to do the work but Bo. Mr. Olivera let him lie on the library rug and read whatever he wanted. At least he didn't make a nuisance of himself. I watched him out of the corner of my eye as he flipped through a *National Geographic* Mr. Olivera had pulled the naked pictures from. Later, he started a *Hardy Boys* mystery. He seemed genuinely lost in the book, and every so often his tail would twitch like he might have come to a good part. He didn't even hear the bell for recess.

Mr. Olivera used his kindest voice. "Son, time to go out and play."

Bo heaved himself off the floor. I followed as he shambled to the swings where Rhonda waited. Some demon-magic lifted them off the ground in high arcs. They didn't even have to pump their legs.

Most of Rhonda's class and mine gathered around them, chanting:

Rhonda and Bo
Sitting in a tree
K-I-S-S-I-N-G

The words were truly a curse. When the bell rang and they came to a stop, Rhonda leaned over and kissed Bo right on the lips.

On the way home, Bo took my place on the bus next to Rhonda, holding hands with her.

Mr. Teddy scolded them. "Cut it out. You're too young to be boyfriend and girlfriend."

Bo put his arm around Rhonda's shoulder. I brooded next to a second grade girl with a drippy nose and decided I'd do what Daddy often accused Mommy of and give them both the Silent Treatment.

As we got off the bus, Rhonda stood with her lunchbox at her side, waiting for my goodbye. I didn't say, "See you later, Alligator," as I'd done every day since kindergarten. Instead, I clenched my teeth. Bo and Rhonda could share kisses and every gummy devil in the universe if they wanted. I didn't care.

I felt my first demon enter me as I walked away. I didn't know what it was, but it felt like a worm nibbling at my heart.

Five Card Stud

When I got home, the garage door gaped open. Daddy leaned on the freezer, staring across at the wall where his hammers and wrenches hung. He clenched a shot glass with his old friend Jim Beam perched behind him.

Bo caught up to me, panting. "Daddy broke the promise he made to you, didn't he?"

I hissed. "Don't you dare call him Daddy."

"Can if I want."

Bo stuck out his tongue, walked into the garage and gave Daddy a hug. He rested his head on Daddy's belly. "I love you the way you are."

Daddy ruffed his hair. I'd lost my status of being his favorite.

When I was about four, we visited Grandma in Indiana. I barely remembered anything about being there except for sitting at her dining table with the horror of lamb and green mint jelly congealing on my tongue. My jealousy tasted the same way.

I used the front door to come into the house, so I didn't have to pass by them. Mommy stood at the kitchen counter cutting a cucumber so fast I was afraid she'd chop off one of her fingers.

"I hate that man, Charlotte. Not even noon, and he started to drink again."

Bo came in through the door from the garage. "You're too ashamed to raise us on welfare, aren't you? Too bad you don't have any job skills."

Within a moment, Bo grew as tall as Mommy. His freckles gave way to pimples, not as bad as Jason's acne but impressive nonetheless. He reeked of Daddy's Old Spice after-shave.

"If I could only take care of the three of you." Mommy attacked a tomato. "I wouldn't make enough money working at a dime store. I've never done anything else."

"And traffic is so bad in Vegas, isn't it, Mommy?" Bo put an arm around her shoulder. She stopped chopping and leaned against him. "You might get killed if you drove. Or worse." He raised his eyebrows in horror. "You might kill one of us."

Time for someone to be practical here. "I bet Millie would help you learn to drive."

Bo shot me a look screaming *Smarty Pants*. "Millie's too busy."

"Millie's too busy, honey." Mommy took a can opener from the drawer and hooked it on the lid of a soup can. She smiled at me. "Chicken noodle, your favorite."

A few minutes later, Connie stormed into the house. She threw her books on the living room floor and headed straight toward Bo.

"You shithead. How could you do this to me?"

Bo shrank into his eight-year-old whiny self, covering his head with his pudgy arms. "Mommy, Connie's picking on me."

Connie tried to kick him but missed and almost lost her footing. She grabbed onto me to keep from falling. "He's spreading lies about me at school."

Bo appeared at Dwight Eisenhower while at the same time twitching his tail to the *Hardy Boys* in my class? How could he be two ages and in two places at the same time, kissing Rhonda on a swing while he ruined my sister's reputation?

Mommy cranked the can opener's handle for the last time and pulled the lid away. "Calm down, Connie. What happened?"

"Bo told everyone—"

Daddy carried in the sweet whiskey scent from the garage. My gut clenched in radar warning.

Bo stood at attention, his arms by his side like a little soldier of chaos. "Connie fooled around with Freeman at the carnival. I went to get a drink from the fountain at the back of the gym and found them lip-locked behind the bleachers." Bo's eyes became saucers. "Daddy, Freeman's hands were in places they shouldn't have been."

The heat of Daddy's anger burned along my spine. "You ...little...tramp."

Daddy took off his belt.

Mommy moved in front of Connie. "You'll have to use it on me first."

Maybe Daddy would notice me and stop. Maybe my body had a force field to protect them. Daddy had never hurt either Connie or me because he loved us. He'd come to his senses any minute and figure out Bo lied.

Connie covered her hands with her mouth and spoke through them. "I didn't do anything. You know that, Daddy. You were there. You took my picture."

I possessed no force field. I offered no protection. The belt left stripes on Connie's legs, but Mommy took the worst of it. After Daddy snapped the belt several times, he dropped it. Then as though he were waking from a nightmare, a great sob escaped from his gut and he fled back into the garage. A few moments later, he drove off.

Bo walked up to the door and closed it. He studied the three of us as we held each other. I put my cheek on Mommy's dress and dampened it with tears.

Were Bo's eyes glistening? The little creep had a conscience?

If so, his remorse lasted less than a few seconds. He gave me the finger and ran out of the room.

Connie shook with sobs.

Mommy pulled away from her. "I wish your father would die."

Connie abruptly stopped crying, as though she turned to stone from one second to the next. "Then do something, Mom. You take whatever he does to you. And now you expect me to? Get us out of here."

Mommy's skin was splotchy, and her cheeks had grown puffy. She squeezed her forehead tight like she was trying hard to push her feelings away.

"Connie, I will protect you and Charlotte as much as I can. But I am caught." She dumped the contents of the soup can into the pot resting on the stove, and a nasty sense of satisfaction filled me. She didn't mention Bo. "Your job is to grow up and get yourselves educated so that you don't end up like me. Until then, I will protect you with my life."

I leaned against Connie and held my breath along with her, exhaling when she did. She put her arm around me. "You think you're protecting us? Come on, Charlotte."

Connie led me into our bathroom and turned on the faucet. I didn't want to wash away my tears. I didn't want to feel better, but I splashed water on my eyes anyway.

She patted my face dry with the hand towel. "As soon as I can, I'm leaving here."

But that meant I'd be alone in the house without a fully human sibling. "Can I come with you?"

She shook her head. "You'll have to figure things out for yourself. That's the way it is, Charlotte. It's how life works."

"Well, life can jerk off."

Connie giggled and put her hand over my mouth. "Where did you hear that word?"

The "j" word?

"From Jason."

Connie put down the towel. "Do you know what jerk off means?"

I didn't, but I refused to admit it. "Yes."

"No, you don't."

My sister whispered in my ear. My eyes grew wide in the mirror.

Mommy announced the soup was ready.

Bo answered in a sugary voice, "Not hungry, Mommy."

Bo not hungry? Sure enough, when Connie and I went to the kitchen, he stretched back in the recliner with a package of Oreos in his lap.

I wanted to call him a jerk-off so badly my teeth hurt as they clenched the words back into my throat.

When Mommy put me to bed that night, she told me we needed a heart-to-heart. First, she promised to give me earplugs for when she and Daddy had a fight, but then she got to what she wanted to say.

"I know it's hard for you, Doll Baby, but what happened this afternoon isn't Rhonda's business, you understand? If anyone asks about Connie, you say she isn't feeling well."

Not an issue. I'd planned on giving Rhonda the Silent Treatment anyway. Mommy kissed me good night and went out to watch Peyton Place. Neither Connie nor I'd been allowed to see it, but Connie asked if she could stay up.

Mommy never relented about this sort of thing, but this time she did. "I guess for tonight, it's okay."

As soon as the theme song came on, I got out of bed and fed Goldie.

"Don't you get tired swimming in the same circle?"

I wanted to believe she wiggled her back fin to tell me about her absolute contentment.

I checked inside the Herman's Hermits album. The matchbook rested snugly between the record and the cover. I didn't want to go back to Hell. Ever. I slipped it back in and climbed into bed, falling into an uneasy sleep with Rhonda's paper burning my ear beneath my pillow.

⇝⇝ ⇜⇜

When I arrived at the bus stop the next morning, Jason was the only kid there. The desert can be cold in winter. He sat hunched in his jacket, white steam puffing from his mouth.

"Where's Connie?"

Connie had big welts on her legs. I repeated what Mommy told me to say. "She's sick."

A couple of junior high boys wandered up. They started kicking each other and slamming their books on each other's heads.

Since I had Jason to myself, I had to find out what had happened with him and Bo. "What did you and Bo do on Sunday?"

Jason looked down the road. No bus, so he had to talk to me.

"Your brother's a freak. We were going to turn trash cans over, but then he wigged out on me. He wanted to torch a shed out on Valley View, and then he started talking trash about Connie."

"Like what?"

"He wanted me to tell my friends I'd gotten to second base with her."

"But Connie hates baseball."

Jason shook his head at my ignorance. Well, I had some news for him.

"You have a picture of Connie in your sock drawer."

Jason flushed red. "Remind me to kill Rhonda." Other kids had arrived and were milling about now. He lowered his voice. "I swear to God, Charlotte, I wouldn't do anything to hurt Connie." His bus pulled up, and he got off the bench. "Bo must have gotten Freeman to say something because there's a rumor spreading about the two of them."

Ok, time to play my hand. "Bo's a demon."

"You're telling me."

"Jason, I'm not kidding. He really is from Hell."

Jason smirked and climbed up the steps.

As soon as the bus disappeared down the street, Bo appeared in the spot Jason had vacated, this time as his third-grade self. His lips were blue and his teeth chattered.

Bo hugged himself. "Daddy Abaxas told me my new home would be in a warm place. I hate Earth."

Rhonda wandered up the sidewalk staring at the concrete. I studied my boots. When she got closer, I deliberately got up and walked to the curb with my back to the bench.

"Hi, Bo. Oh, chocolate with sprinkles. Thank you."

Happiness filled Rhonda's voice. I became more aware of the demon taking hold of me, an ugly thing that may or may not have been sent from Hell. The worm I'd noticed the afternoon before had chewed to the center of my heart and began its residence there.

The smell of diesel surrounded me in an invisible cloud. I spun around to glare at Rhonda as Mr. Tommy's bus hugged the curb.

She held the half-eaten doughnut in her hands, her math book next to her on the bench. I cursed her with the dark power my heart now held.

She dropped the doughnut. Bo put a protective arm around her.

I hated myself for hating her, but I needed to hate someone. Daddy was too scary and Mommy too weak. Connie had disappeared into a strange world unto herself. Rhonda had been my friend, but she'd chosen Bo over me.

I gave up trying to evade the pain of the paper I stole from Hell, which slowly roasted in the pocket of the blue velvet jumper Mommy had sewn for me. I boarded the bus, turned my back on my former friend, and left her in the hands of the demon she loved.

⟫⟫⟩ ⟨⟨⟨⟨

Commercials for the grand opening of Burning Sands Casino broadcast on all of the stations, even the evening news from places like New York and Washington D.C. Underlings passed through my bedroom from the time the TV turned off until just before Mommy's alarm rang. They carried boxes and bar stools. One night they rolled roulette wheels over my carpet, one after another.

Ezequiel passed by my bed and never even whispered, "Hi, Cupcake."

I curled into a ball of despair, but I was no longer afraid. Hell could have its stupid casino. What did Burning Sands have to do with me?

The night after the Christmas program at school, Abraxas strolled from my closet. He'd left his Halloween get up, the cape, and the other weird clothes in Hell. He now wore what looked like a fine suit, from what little I knew of fancy men's clothes from lawyer shows, and a dark brown wool winter coat with a matching fedora. We had a few pictures of Daddy wearing a similar one from way back in the 50s.

"Good evening, Charlotte. I know you're not asleep."

No use in pretending. I unwound from my fetal position and sat up.

Abraxas took off his coat and hung it over his left arm. "I trust Bo has been an influence."

"Ask him. Not me."

Abraxas's cat eyes glinted in the dark. Goldie's little scales caught their light so that she glowed softly in her bowl. A growl inside my closet made him turn away from me.

"Quiet them, you fools."

Kamaris and Ezequiel entered, both of them leading tigers on leashes. Suddenly my bravado drained from me. The cats looked very hungry, and I felt very small. The tigers' chuffing Abraxas took Ezequiel's leash ~~and purring~~ made my room vibrate. "Kamaris, come with me. Ezequiel, check that tomorrow's shipment is on schedule."

The demon boss and the old goon left my room. Ezequiel squatted next to my bed. His halo seemed dull, even in the slant light of my nightlight.

"I haven't been able to talk to you. They're watching the underlings closely right now."

I said the meanest thing possible. "I hope the tigers poop in the living room, and you have to clean it up."

My words had the opposite effect than I wanted. Ezequiel chuckled. He took both of my hands, palm to palm, as though I prayed, and held them between his. His horns sparked for a second, but their light vanished faster than a match being blown out.

"I'm watching out for you, Charlotte."

"Then play a game of Parcheesi, and you can tell me how that's working."

He stood and glanced back at the closet. "I can't. Not now."

"Figures."

"I'm sorry, but I have to go."

Ezequiel jumped through my closet floor.

I spoke to the echoes of heat floating toward my bed. "Some guardian demon you turned out to be."

⤜⤜⤜⤜   ⤛⤛⤛⤛

Daddy came home Saturday afternoon, totally sober. He'd left late in the morning to go grocery shopping, weird because Mommy and Daddy always did this together, dragging Connie and me along. He yelled for all of us to get into the kitchen, pronto.

Everyone assembled, and he let us in on the mystery.

"I got a job as Head of Security at Burning Sands. Double times on Sundays. Triple time on the holidays. Better pay than at LVPD, so I quit."

If I had been Mommy, I'd have blown a gasket. Instead, she grew pale, and I barely heard her. "Your pension, Walter. You were only ten years away from retiring. What about benefits? You know Charlotte needs braces."

I did?

Daddy's gaze turned into disgust. "Goddamn it, Juney." He'd never called her "Juney" before. "You'd like to put out for Captain Hartinson to keep me on the force, wouldn't you? I got goddamn benefits, and a goddamn pension twice as much as I had working for that jerk."

Connie said what I wanted to. "You're the one who's a jerk, Daddy."

I felt relieved she didn't add the "off."

Daddy ignored her and put a foot on one of the dinette chairs, exposing a holster on his ankle. He still had his service revolver.

"Mr. Abraxas treats me with respect. None of this regulation bullshit the police department dishes out." He slid the gun out, put it on the table, and lowered his leg to the floor. "I'm going to be treated like a real man, not some mannequin in a suit. I get to play undercover for good, but this time for an organization that's going to take care of me."

Connie's pea coat draped over the same chair. She grabbed it and ran out the front door, slamming it behind her.

Mommy ran to the door. "Get back here now." She stood at the door for a good minute and then walked back to us. "What are the neighbors going to think?"

I felt Bo hovering like a rain cloud. He stepped around me and took Daddy's hand. "There's a poker game tonight, isn't there? I'll help you unload the car. I hope you didn't forget the mixed nuts."

Mommy finally lost that gasket. She waved her arms wildly as she started screaming. How dare Daddy accuse her of fooling around. She'd put up with his horse poop for almost fifteen years, and she was tired of it.

Daddy spewed more curse words at her than he ever did before, and that's saying something. I made a promise to myself. I'd never have a boyfriend. I wouldn't let Daddy ever have an excuse to accuse me of anything.

That evening, our poker table sat in the middle of the living room. The Christmas tree lights blinked brightly as though they were ready for a good party. Schlitz, Budweiser, Cokes, Vernors Ginger Ale, and orange juice filled our refrigerator. Four bottles of Jim Beam and a couple of Smirnoff took up the space on the counter next to the sink. Everyone at the table smoked cigarettes or cigars. Tomorrow morning, I'd be on the ashtray patrol.

Mommy had told me to go to my room and to stay there, but after she disappeared into hers I tiptoed back in. I watched the game from the couch with a big glass filled with ice and ginger ale.

Abraxas wore his beautiful suit. Bo put his head on his real father's shoulder, rocking back and forth in his house shoes, clutching his demon teddy which wore a Santa's hat. Teddy kept looking at Abraxas's cards until Abraxas shook Bo off.

Bo squeezed the bear so hard I thought the button along his tummy would pop. He put his arm around Daddy's shoulder, and Daddy kissed the top of Bo's head.

Kamaris dressed the same casual way Daddy did, loose dark blue polyester trousers big men seemed to wear with shirts that almost made them look like twins, except Daddy's was olive green and Kamaris wore black. Kamaris had planted his bare feet firmly on the floor, if you called his fleshy appendages feet. At least nothing squishy oozed onto the carpet.

The doorbell rang. A couple of patrolmen from the precinct who'd always come to Daddy's other poker parties walked in, both of them holding brown bags with more booze.

The house game at the Jackson's was Five Card Stud. Daddy had been on a winning streak by the time Mark and Chuck sat down. Abraxas shuffled the deck, but before he dealt he held up a shot glass of amber liquid.

"To a fruitful enterprise." Everyone else raised their glasses. He turned toward me. "Join us in a toast, Charlotte."

I pulled my knees up as if I could hide behind them. "No, thank you."

Daddy motioned for me with his index finger. "Come on, Charlotte."

Bo took a sip from Daddy's beer.

Connie walked through the door in the nick of time. She'd been gone for hours. She shoved her hands deep in the pockets of her coat while she scanned the living room. I set my glass on the coffee table and hurried to her. Connie smelled smoky too.

Daddy called after me. "Hey, get back here."

Abraxas raised his left hand. Everyone at the table froze.

"Don't bother, Walt."

Abraxas lowered his hand to the table. The men moved again.

Daddy threw a blue chip into the pot. "Good night, girls."

Connie pulled me down the hall.

"Stay out of there, you hear me? At school everyone is saying Burning Sands is run by the mob."

The threat of meat grinders hadn't crossed my mind for months. "Aren't all of the casinos?"

Connie shook her head. "This time it's different. The main guy who runs it seems to be from some foreign place and rumor has it he's worse than the rest." She pushed me into my room. "Lock your door."

I didn't mention that the main guy was laying down bets in our living room. "But we're not allowed to—"

"Lock it, Charlotte."

Doors to the outside of the house were always latched, not the ones inside. But I did what she said. The unfamiliar sound of the click made me feel safer, but I had to remember to unlock it before Mommy got up.

Behind me, a woman spoke. "Nice to see you again, kiddo."

I turned to see the Virgin of the Screen Door sitting in my desk chair, a go-go boot on her left foot. Her feet looked pretty big, but it fit.

"You're not going to want these anymore. No one will be wearing them after the first of the year."

She squeezed her right foot into my other boot, and then ran her hands over both from her toes up to her calves. The boots turned dark brown and extended to her knees. High heels popped from the back of the soles like switchblades.

She'd nailed it. None of the girls at school were wearing the boots anymore except for Rhonda—and me.

Ezequiel had called her Lily. Lily wore a royal blue mini-dress. Her straight black hair fell to her hips. Connie's hair, even when she had Mommy iron it, always kept a bit of a wave. My sister would be envious if she'd ever met her. She stood and took two long strides to my closet and turned around like she'd had training as a model.

Laughter broke out from the poker party. Lily shook her head. "Them guys."

I had a burning question. "Why were you on the screen door at the Garcias?"

She glanced toward the ceiling. "Mary lets me fill in for her from time to time when she's busy. The On-High doesn't seem to mind. I think Mary feels sorry for me. You know, she might have gone down my wicked path, if things hadn't worked out so well for her."

"What do you mean?"

"When you get a bad reputation, it's hard to shake. Bless her heart, Mary's a nice girl. She deserves to be the Mother of God."

"I don't understand any of that stuff."

"Well, it's complicated. The thing is, I get these visions of Heaven from time to time. Maybe from hanging out with her when she decides to take a break from the hosannas. It almost hurts knowing I'm never going to see Heaven for real. I did bad things, Charlotte, but once, believe it or not, I used to be a little girl like you."

Johnny Horton began to sing *The Mansion You Stole* from the living room. Daddy had each record he ever made. We mourned when the news announced his death and went to the drive-in to see *North to Alaska* in honor of him. Where did Johnny wind up, I wondered.

Lily's smile looked tired. "I'd better get myself in there." She sang a little ditty about boots that were made for walking.

"Catchy."

"You think?"

She put her hand on the door knob. Click, it unlocked. "Hey, Charlotte. I know you got that paper."

Geez. Did all the demons know my secrets?

"You have choices. Don't end up like me, ok?"

I nodded, not sure what she meant.

"Well, time to provide the entertainment. You lock this door behind me, okay?"

I nodded again.

When she left, I turned out the light and crawled under my covers. Rain started to fall and hit the roof like the hooves of reindeer I'd started to have doubts about.

A few minutes later, Bo tapped on my door.

"Charlotte, let me in."

"No way."

"Please, I'll play Parcheesi with you."

Well, why not?

Demon Teddy slept in the crook of Bo's arm smelling as though he had a lot more than one sip of Daddy's beer.

"Did your teddy take a bath in booze?"

Bo hiccupped. "I couldn't stop him."

I got the game out of my closet. A minute later, I shook my cup. I rolled a five right off and moved my first piece from the nest.

Bo put a thumb in his mouth, so I scolded him. "Take that out of your mouth. Aren't you like three thousand years old?"

"Much older." He shook his cup. "Daddy Abraxas says I grow wider, but I don't grow up."

"What about when you went to Connie's school and ruined her reputation?"

He rolled a three and a four. Smoke trickled from his ears. "Thirteen is as old as I ever get."

My turn again. Another five. "You do realize I hate you."

"I'm doing what Daddy Abraxas wants me to do, Charlotte. You're not perfect, you know."

The worm nestled in my heart. I touched my chest. The temperature rose, and I broke out in a sweat. Bo rolled snake eyes.

Ezequiel appeared in the room, his black leather jacket looked dusty and his Little Joe hair a mess.

"Can I join the two of you?"

Not that easy.

"Next game, Ezequiel."

He lowered himself gracefully to the floor and watched Bo and I play three whole games before I let him in on the action. Lily's voice filtered through my wall from time to time, a reprieve from the laughter and cursing from the big game of Five Card Stud.

The three of us played quietly until Bo asked a question just as the sun was rising. "There's something I need to know. Is Santa Claus real?"

And Aways We Go: 1968

Kids at school had been calling me Gorilla Girl since sixth grade because I didn't shave my legs. I begged Mom over and over to let me, but despite what I saw as a forest from my knees to my ankles, she insisted I was too young. I don't know why Rhonda told her mom I was being teased, but a quarter way through seventh grade Millie had a heart-to-heart with Mom. She convinced her to let me take this step in growing up. A small step, perhaps, but my new smooth shins felt like sophistication itself.

Connie, of course, never asked permission to do anything. When she came home one afternoon after piercing her ears with a needle and an ice cube at a friend's house, the argument between them made me feel if the world came to an end before bedtime, I'd welcome it.

Mom's anger at my sister for pushing the limits made me cautious. Connie and I existed in completely different realms in Mom's mind. Connie would always be difficult, and I'd be her baby forever. She told me more than once she counted on me to not add to her worries.

Little did she know, right?

I might have been a frequent visitor to Hell, but I didn't have my sister's independent spirit at home, her moxie to wear white lipstick and dye her hair blonde, nor her ability to take risks. She'd even managed to stay alive after Daddy caught her necking with Freeman on our front porch when he came home unexpectedly one night from the casino. The terrible scene left me shaken. I think it fueled Connie's desire to do anything she damned well wanted.

And Rhonda? No matter how crappy I treated her, the older she became the more likely she turned the other cheek, habitually showering kindnesses. Her goodness irked me. Sometimes I suspected Rhonda had a sixth sense about what she was doing.

I'd begun to carry her paper in my left shoe, a better location than a pocket or scorching my sensitive parts. It burned hotter with each new caring act, while the worm grew hungrier and chewed bigger chunks out of my heart.

Emptiness hurts. A lot.

I'd hoped for a Bo-less year at school when I went to junior high. And, of course, my hopes were dashed. Teachers considered my brother a genius. I worked my butt off and barely managed a B average. He never did anything, and his report cards magically filled with As semester after semester. Pushed ahead, he skipped a grade.

When Bo and I got home from school one Tuesday, we found Daddy sitting at the head of the table with our places set around big buckets of Kentucky Fried Chicken, mashed potatoes, and a plate of dinner rolls as the centerpiece. Cheerful red Coke cans decorated the table.

"Early dinner, kiddos, before I go to work. We're celebrating."

I bought a Snickers at the 7-11 on the way home. The smell of the chicken made my stomach queasy.

Daddy gave Bo a quick kiss and piled a bunch of chicken thighs, a mountain of mashed potatoes, and three dinner rolls on his plate. Bo headed to the recliner without even a thank you. He never missed *Dark Shadows*.

Daddy smiled at his beautiful baby boy dragging his fat ass into the living room and then turned toward me with a soft look on his face. He patted my hand.

Mom had been on the phone in their room. She sat down and pinched her mouth into a tight line. "Connie got into trouble for smoking again at school."

Daddy plopped some potatoes on his plate. "I'll stop by on the way to work."

Since working at Burning Sands, he had a way with people. No doubt he'd charm Miss Finklestein, the principal, whom he called Miss Spinsterstein behind her back. Connie wouldn't be suspended.

Daddy raised his Coke. "A toast."

We clinked cans.

Mom kept her hands in her lap. "So, Walter, what's this shindig about?"

"I busted Roger O'Malley, the city councilman, the one who tried to pull the fast one on Mr. Abraxas." Daddy set his drink down and motioned for my plate. "O'Malley threatened that if the casino didn't share a little revenue with him, he'd make the boss's life tough." He plopped a mountain of potatoes next to the roll I'd chosen and handed the plate back. The Snickers churned in my stomach. "Grab yourself a drumstick, Charlotte."

Fake screams echoed from the TV.

Mom walked into the living room, turned the volume down and then came back. "And?"

"That sap didn't know who he was dealing with." Did Daddy mean Abraxas or himself? "So, I set him up with this floozy. Got pictures of the two of them carrying on near the slots and then slipping off into a room. I convinced him I was another customer of that broad. Perfect sting."

Mom's brows came together. "You used to be a cop, Walter. You used to stand for something."

"My sting worked. For Burning Sands. And, by the way, for the LVPD." Each of Daddy's words felt like a punch. "That SOB Hartman and I had a little talk. I might be helping out the force from time to time for a little extra dough, so don't you get high and mighty with me. Once a cop, always a cop, even if I don't have a badge no longer."

Mom stared at Daddy above her empty plate as he kept talking.

"You're not going to tell me you won't enjoy spending the extra cash I'm bringing in. They're even mentioning my name in the Sun with a picture of Hartman shaking my hand. So keep your fat mouth shut, Juney, and don't start acting like Millie with her goddamn Canuck boyfriend she's shacking up with." Mom tapped her shoe The sole of her Mom's tapped rapidly on the floor. They'd bicker until he left. I glanced at the clock. When Connie got home, I'd lay money there'd be a scene between her and mom. A 90 percent chance, I figured.

I took two bites from my drumstick. If I ate more, there'd be a 100 percent chance of my puking. I got up, threw the chicken in the trash, and scraped the potatoes in the garbage disposal.

In the living room, I walked over to Bo and knelt next to the recliner. "Would you cover for me?"

Daddy and Mom's voices rose. Bo clicked the remote and turned the volume as high as it would go. "Why should I?"

"Come on, Bo. I need to get out of here."

His horns wiggled. He kept staring at the TV. "Then you treat Rhonda better, or you won't know what pain is."

"I want to be nice to her. I honestly do." A quick sharp jolt shot up my leg. "You don't understand how hard it is."

Bo mimicked my whine. "You don't understand." A commercial came on, and he gave me his complete attention.

Was that fuzz on his cheeks?

"I can't believe you haven't figured this out by now. I understand everything."

I took a sip of the Coke I'd brought with me. It tasted warm.

"Look, I promise to be a better friend to Rhonda. Plus, if you let me disappear for a while, I won't tell her you sleep with your teddy."

Smoke puffed out of his horns.

"Deal. I don't know why you hang out with that loser."

Loser meaning Ezequiel, who languished in the filing department now the casino was up and running. Abraxas lived full time in Vegas. A stream of goons and demons of every rank waltz through my bedroom most nights, and they never made a return trip. On occasion, Karmiris would slurp from the other direction, leading regretful Burning Sands clients who'd sold their souls for a big spin on the roulette wheel or the perfect blackjack game. They lived it up for a month, and then the bill came due. Chances were I'd see Mr. City Councilman paraded through one day.

A few minutes later with my matchbook in my pocket, I strolled through the halls on my way to the filing room. Eyes in the walls quivered, but I no longer jumped when they snapped open. I was a regular now.

Ezequiel stashed a skeleton key to Room 777 in a niche above the door where an eye had fallen out. I fingered it out of the hole and unlocked the door which made its familiar nails-on-a-blackboard squeak as I opened it. I stepped quickly through the front room to the files and found Ezequiel leaning over the cart, sorting through the bin.

As usual, there didn't seem to be a method to his system. He picked up random handfuls of papers and dealt them back like they were a deck of cards.

He climbed into the cart's seat. "Hey, I hoped you might show up tonight."

I hopped in next to him, and we headed down the tracks.

"Remember when I told you about Millie's new boyfriend? Mom thinks it's romantic, him being from a foreign country." I took a fingernail and fished out a bit of chicken from between my teeth. "But I don't think she approves. She said Catholics can get away with a lot more than the rest of us. Find a priest and confess," I snapped my fingers, "and poof, sin forgiven."

Ezequiel's response had an edge. "That easy, huh?"

The cart slowed, stopping at the Naa-Nix section.

He'd always been touchy about the forgiveness thing, but I'd been wanting to ask him something for quite a while. Since I'd brought the subject up, I figured I might as well go for it.

"Do you think if the priest got to the accident in time to give you last rites, you'd be in Heaven now?"

Ezequiel put the brake on and stared at the long line of rails disappearing in the darkness. "You're really asking me?"

I folded my left leg beneath me and turned so I saw his whole face. "I'm not Catholic, remember. No chance for a priest when I die. Yes, I'm asking you."

His fingers drummed on the bar in front of him for an uncomfortably long time. Had I stepped over the line? He pushed himself from the seat and walked around to my side. I jumped out.

He picked up one of the papers at the top and stared at it. "There are things you can never be forgiven for."

In the three years I'd known him, we'd only skirted the topic of that awful night in New Mexico. I'd asked questions, and he'd clam up.

I shifted my feet and put my hand on his, circling his knuckles as he grasped the paper. "You didn't mean to kill your sister. You were stupid, not evil, Ezequiel. You don't deserve to be punished for an eternity."

He yanked his hand away. The paper flew into the canyon of cabinets at our side.

"Damn it." The light of Ezequiel's halo sputtered as though it had blown a fuse. His horns scattered black soot. I'd never seen him this angry. "How old do I look? Tell me the truth, Charlotte."

I stared at the huge pile of sin in the back of the cart. "Like a senior in high school?"

I glanced up. His eyes were shiny.

"I've been dead for over fifteen years. I haven't aged a day. In a few years, you're going to be older than me, get out of the hellhole you live in and have a life. I'm going to be stuck here dropping these papers into these damn files when you're an old woman. And you know what? I deserve it. I took Joanne's life."

I swallowed hard. Little splinters of sadness poked me inside and the tears came.

He sniffed and glanced away. "Don't cry. I can't stand it when girls cry. Stay here, will you?"

Ezequiel walked around the hanging ladder and disappeared between the cabinets. I blew my nose on the hem of my shirt and read a couple of random papers.

Heinrich Naegeli, born December 2, 1948, kicked his dog, broke a rib.

Latricia Bowlin Nayers, born April 14, 1935, told a lie to her sister, Arletta Bowlin, born July 26, 1938, about why she wasn't coming to Thanksgiving Dinner with their parents.

How shocked I'd been when I discovered every white lie told on Earth was recorded. Who'd ever get into Heaven? Now, a jaded twelve-year-old, I tossed Latricia back in the bin and wished her luck.

Another paper stung my fingers when I touched it. I licked my thumb and forefinger and gingerly picked it up.

Richard Nixon, born January 9, 1913. Told you he's our guy.

I dropped the President-Elect's sins before I read anymore and piled a bunch of papers on top of them.

Ezequiel came huffing back with the stray paper wadded in his right hand.

I leaned back on the cart and crossed my arm. "I want to know more about Joanne. I think if you talked about her, you'd feel better."

He threw down the crumpled paper and grabbed the rim of the cart with both hands, bowing his head. "No one was kinder than Joanne."

"And?"

"And that's it."

"Ezequiel!"

"Not now, Charlotte. Tell me Millie's boyfriend's name again. Didn't it start with an N?"

"You're trying to distract me."

Ezequiel's mouth bent into a little smile. "Guilty."

I uncrossed my arms. "Hayden Nelson."

Ezequiel sunk his hand into the bin and fished out a paper. His sorting system worked like a charm. "What does this guy do?"

"Deals blackjack at the Golden Nugget."

Rhonda's paper burned hotter than it ever had. I lifted my heel to try to get relief. I'd tried a dozen times to put the paper in Rhonda's file on my visits to Hell, but it always came back.

At my tenth birthday party, my presents were wrapped in multiple copies, though, of course, everyone else saw flowers and balloons and frilly ribbons.

When my family passed through Salt Lake City on vacation, I dropped the paper in a trash can at the Mormon Tabernacle, but the next morning I woke up dreaming of seagulls taking bites out of me and found Rhonda's day from so long ago wadded in my fist, bits of steam seeping through my clenched fingers.

Once I got desperate enough and ate the paper, but my stomach immediately cramped. It materialized the next day in my underwear.

I accept I'd never rid myself of the trespass I'd committed or the crummy worm of resentment infecting me.

Ezequiel unfolded Nelson Hayden's paper and scanned it. "Canada Man is a real professional."

"What do you mean? Millie and he aren't star-crossed, are they?"

"You're reading Shakespeare?"

I shook my head. "Not yet. But when Connie read *Romeo and Juliet* she got very dramatic and kept saying she'd stick daggers in her—" I paused, suddenly embarrassed. The word "breast" wouldn't leave my mouth. I felt my cheeks redden. "In her chest."

I pretended to plunge a dagger into mine.

"You should be on Broadway, Charlotte." Ezequiel read more. "This Nelson fellow's been married four times. He spent yesterday morning on the phone with two of his ex-wives. And it looks like he has connections your father would be interested in."

"What do you mean?"

Ezequiel handed the paper to me. *Card shark. Try to recruit to Burning Sands. Much promise.*

Earth. Such a sad place. My mom and dad suffered. So did Millie, Hayden, grumpy teachers, politicians, and the millions of lives held by the files in this cavernous room. Everyone alive or dead had been a kid like me once. My shoulders dropped from weariness.

"What's up, Cupcake?" I didn't flinch at the nickname. He pulled me to him and kissed the top of my head. Brother-like.

I wished the kiss had felt differently.

"Do you think that the On-High has someone filing for him? Putting the good stuff down?"

He didn't answer. A large clunking sound, metal rubbing against metal banged around us. The room seemed to inhale. I waited for the exhalation, but it never came. The air conditioning turned off, and the temperature shot up.

Kamaris's voice rolled down the track like a shock wave. "Hey, girly. I knows you're here."

Ezequiel shoved me behind him. "Get out of here now."

I pulled out the matchbook. Three left. I struck one. It sputtered and went out. The next did the same. If I'd been Mom, I'd have muttered, "Sugarfoot," but a word much more fitting for my surroundings came out of my mouth.

"Ezequiel, you didn't say these had an expiration date."

"They're not supposed to."

Before I had a chance to light the last one, Kamaris pointed a long finger in our direction. "I knows you're here, little girly, and you and your boyfriend are comings with me." He planted himself three feet from the cart. I peeked around Ezequiel's back. "Young lady, I knows what you tooks out of here."

Sharp pain shot up my ankle. I slipped the last match in my pocket and stepped next to Ezequiel, putting my hand on his arm for balance and pulled off my shoe. I took out Rhonda's paper and unfolded it. The creases were deep. Resentment for her rose like bile in my throat.

Ezequiel looked at me in disbelief. "I told you never to take anything out of here."

"I took it on my first visit."

My excuse was pitiable.

"You kept this from me?"

Now I'd plunged daggers into him twice, bringing up Joanne and then having him discover I'd betrayed him. I thrust the paper at Kimaris. "I don't want it anymore. I wanted to show off, but I've paid for taking it."

Kimaris threw up both of his webbed hands. "I'm not touching that thing. When the Abraxas finds out, I don't wants him to think I hads anything to do with it."

He slung me over his shoulder, slithering back over the tracks with speed I'd never have imagined he'd be capable of. Ezequiel left the cart behind, following us, slipping and sliding on the goo Kimaris exuded.

I writhed.

I kicked.

I screamed, "Let me go," over and over.

When we reached the door to the hallway, Kimaris dropped me on the hard floor.

He wagged his finger. "Nows, you be quiet."

Ezequiel reached us, breathing hard, as Kimaris opened the door. Across the hall, the door for Room 778 flung open, a woman with thick spectacles low on her nose stood in the threshold looking bewildered.

Kimaris took one step toward her. "You minds your own business. Go backs to the traffic tickets."

The woman slammed her door so fast the paisley print of her dress caught in the crack.

"Humans. I thoughts it was a bad idea to makes them into underlings and puts them to work down here, but does anyones ever listens to me?" Kimaris motioned us forward. "This ways."

We followed. He pointed his finger at any eyeball that happened to be opened. They snapped shut. The hallway stopped at an elevator. Kimaris pushed the button. Doors opened and we stepped inside.

A mechanical voice reverberated around us. "Going down?"

Karimis grunted. "Very funny."

Ezequiel's halo cast a pale light. The ride became bumpy like the turbulence in airplane movies. I grabbed his arm, and Ezequiel pulled me to him. The elevator slammed to an abrupt stop. The door slid open to a platform jutting into the antonym of Niagara Falls. Walls of falling lava a hundred feet high surrounded us on three sides. Molten rock flowed with black obsidian veins and arteries blazed orange and crimson.

I had to strain to hear Kamaris shout.

"This is the Monotheistic Hell, but I'm tolds the Bardos are equally as impressive." He pointed to another platform below us. A couple of demons, more reptilian than human, swung a man in a business suit by the arms and legs. "One, two, three. And aways we go."

Did Kimaris think he was Jackie Gleason?

The demons tossed the man into the flames. I only glanced at where he landed, but I didn't need to look any longer for the horror to imprint on my mind. Would I end up writhing and contorting like the tortured souls below my feet?

Kimaris snapped his fingers. We now sat in plastic chairs in a cafeteria with ice in our glasses of Coke.

"Welcomes to Purgatory."

Tables extended into the depths of the cafeteria. Hapless souls bent their heads over trays of mashed potatoes, stringy roast beef, and overcooked peas.

Ezequiel didn't look relieved. "What if we're seen here?"

"The Old Guy? He's forgotten about this joint, and that dandy Abraxas wouldn't be caughts dead in a place like this. So, Charlotte, it's likes this."

I felt slimy with my name in his mouth.

"I needs two tickets to the Frank Sinatra show at the Burnings Sands, and since I caughts the twos of you together, you're gonna helps me get them."

I Say A Little Prayer

Kimaris reached into his vest pocket and drew out a picture. "This is my girlfriend, Lily, and she loves Ol' Blue Eyes. She desires to goes with me to the concert."

Coke fizzed up my nose. Lily wanted to date this goon?

My mind flashed on the afternoon of New Year's Eve, the year before. Propped up in bed with my pillows behind my back, I'd been drawing Ezequiel, coloring his leather jacket the coolest shade of purple with my magic pen, when my closet rumbled and hiccupped.

I closed my journal. Who'd be arriving at 3 p.m. for the night's celebration at the Burning Sands?

Lily, that's who. She stepped out in a sparkly gold dress, matching high heels and handbag. Black gloves enveloped her arms to her elbows. She'd swept up her long hair in a graceful French Twist. Mom never wore hers that way again after the fight with Daddy when he grabbed it and she dropped the whiskey bottle.

"Hi, Charlotte. I needed to get out of that dump early." She pointed to the blue inflatable chair I'd gotten for my birthday. "Can I try it out?"

The dress hugged Lily so tightly I didn't know how she'd sink down, but she managed and looked graceful to boot. She sang a few bars of something new and then put a gloved hand to check her hair in back. "Abe hates that song."

I may have been the first human to hear "I Say a Little Prayer."

"Why perform it then?"

Lily gazed at my poster of Bobby Sherman above my bed. Her attention slowly wandered back to me. She leaned forward as far as her dress allowed. "I do it for me. I say little prayers all of the time."

"Don't you get in trouble?"

Lily scoffed. "It's worth it. Gives me hope someday I'll get out of that joint." She jerked her thumb towards my closet. "I tell you, Charlotte, Hell's emptying out. All the demons who have any clout with Abraxas are heading to Vegas. The Old Guy doesn't have the energy to do anything about it."

She exhaled in a long slow sigh. Her face pinched up.

I wanted to go to her and give her a hug, but I held back. "What's wrong?"

"I'm never getting out. I'm one of the oldest demons, you know?"

Lily took off her gloves and put them in her lap as she sang, Bright red polish adorned her nails, which curled like claws. She'd kept them trimmed the other times we spent together. It made me wonder about her toenails. Were they curled and squished in her shoes?

I studied her hands until she lifted her left one and wiped the corner of her eye with her knuckle.

"Abraxas made me grow these things so I wouldn't forget my past. I'm never going to be forgiven."

"For what? You and Ezequiel are the nicest—" Ezequiel didn't have demon status. "—residents of Hell I've met."

She leaned back in the chair and somehow managed to cross her legs. "Do you have time for a long sad story?"

"Sure, Mom and Connie went to the grocery store. Daddy left for work an hour ago."

"You might think differently about me, but I need to get a load off my chest."

During the next hour, I learned about the city of Sumer, where she lived as a poor girl selling trinkets at the base of ziggurats. She then was chosen to be a priestess at the temple.

I had no idea what a ziggurat was, but being a priestess sounded like fun. "Cool."

Her face fell into a shadow. A stale odor filled my room. The air tasted ancient.

"Do you know what job temple priestesses did?" She must have read my blank expression. "What do you know about sex?"

"Everything. Connie's filled me in."

Kinda sorta.

Eating lunch on the bench at school, girls told one fantastic story after another, things older sisters or cousins told them. For some of them, Heaven forbid, their brothers had filled them in. Connie's information about blow jobs appeared to be accurate. I squealed in disgust with the rest of the girls when that particular subject came up, while also feeling strange in the place Mom had said never to touch.

As Lily told her story, I had a hard time maintaining my worldly composure. By the time she finished, my knowledge of possible sins had expanded by quite a lot.

"God, I'm such a wretch. I shouldn't have said anything."

She broke into sobs and bit into a knuckle. Her mascara pooled into black puddles. I handed her the tissue box resting on my nightstand next to Goldie.

Lily blew her nose.

"I'm sure the On-High would have forgiven me, but I did worse things. Stories about me multiplied and became darker. And when I died, I became the stories. I became a demon."

The weight of the air pressed down on us. Her shame paralleled my own for being a bitch to Rhonda. And for looking at Lisa's answers during the math final. And for the dreams I'd been having about Ezequiel based on the tales at lunch. I didn't like the squirminess inside my body.

"But you did those things so long ago. Why not become Catholic and repent?"

She patted her eyes until she resembled a raccoon, but she finally smiled with her oh so white teeth. "That boat sailed long after my time on Earth, darling."

Ezequiel broke me out of my reverie.

"In your dreams Lily's your girlfriend, Kimaris. Besides, why don't you ask Abraxas for some tickets?"

He drained his Coke in one swallow. The glass immediately filled again as though there were an invisible spigot floating above the table.

Kimaris snorted. "Because goons aren't allowed to shows ourselves in public. We does the hard work. We counts the money. We roughs up the clientele, and who gets most of the contracts signed? We does. Lily says she'd go out with me if I gets the tickets. And I'll shows Abraxas what classy guys goons cans be."

Kimaris pointed at me. His finger had too many joints and pulled against the webbing that joined all of his fingers together.

"Looky heres. If I don't gets them, I'm gonna spills the beans on the two of yous. I knews you've been up to something when I caughts you together when she was little and you blew your top, Angel Boy. The demon waiting insides you sure showed himselfs that time."

I remembered how mad Ezequiel got when Kimaris implied he might be doing something inappropriate with me in Room 777. I didn't understand then, but I was older now and I knew what disgusting thing Kimaris meant.

The goon snapped his fingers again. We were back on the platform. The waterfalls of fire showered around us, hot as ever, but the reptilian demons weren't there. A woman with wild gray hair wandered down the walkway below next to the fiery pit. She sobbed and held her arms around her chest.

Kimaris leaned over the rail and yelled at her. "Go backs to your room. You gots lucky. They wents for a Coke break."

We watch her gingerly step backward and disappear inside a dark arch at the end of the platform.

"Geezes." Kimaris pronounced the G the hard way, probably to keep from accidentally invoking the name of you-know-who. "Every demon worth a grain of salt is leavings Hell, and the Old Guy is oblivious." He gave Ezequiel an appraising look. "I also bets you there is a promotion headed your ways. Staff shortage, if you knows what I mean."

The light from Ezequiel's halo went out. Completely. He touched it. "It doesn't feel warm anymore."

Kimaris grinned, his teeth as dark as Lily's were white. "Yeah, Abraxas is building himself quites the operation on Earth. Word gets out. Why stays in Hell when you can haves a swimming pool?"

Ezequiel took off his halo. It dissolved in his fingers. My heart crumbled as though the heat had reached inside it and burned everything to ash, everything but the voracious worm. Tears welled and evaporated right out of my eyeballs. My saliva was thick when I swallowed. I wished I'd finished my Coke.

I remember Lily's story about how she'd been a girl like me. What might I be destined for?

"Tell me what I need to do."

Snap. Only Kimaris and I were back at the table.

I grabbed my Coke and drank so fast I burped. "What happened to Ezequiel?"

"As I saids, he gots a promotion, but I haves a bit of privileged information. Your father's gonna gets tickets for the show, and you're gonna steals them for me."

A snowball's chance that would happen.

"Daddy says Frank Sinatra is a little jerk from New Jersey and a two bit mafioso. I wouldn't be surprised if he took the night off on purpose to not be in the same building with him."

"But your mother—" Kimaris pulled a list from his pocket and handed it to me—"likes Old Blue Eyes a lot."

I scanned the paper. Mom fainted in 1948 listening to Frank on the radio at her girlfriend Pamela's house. She went to the movies and watched *Guys and Dolls* four times, and before she married Daddy she owned every copy of *Photoplay* that featured pictures of him.

Did Daddy hate Frank because Mom liked him?

"You know my dad. You play poker with him. Why would you think Daddy would agree to take Mom to the concert?"

Kimaris leaned closer, his finger an inch from my nose. "Keeps your ears open and you'll finds out."

He snapped his fingers one last time, and I found myself sitting on my bed in the dark. My alarm clock said 3:30. I had a science test the next day. I fell onto my pillow knowing I would be lucky to get a C, and only if I stayed awake.

"Do you know most girls think eighteen is the best age to get married? I wonder if Rhonda would be willing to marry me in six years."

I crawled to the wall and switched on the light. Bo sat in my blue chair looking at one of Connie's *Seventeen* magazines.

"What are you doing here?"

"Worrying about you. Mommy and Daddy would be mad if they knew you've been out so late, especially to a place like Hell."

"You would never ruin your cover. They'd see your ugly lump of a tail."

I'd slowly come to the conclusion Bo didn't want things to change. He liked living with the Jackson family and being a pest.

During Christmas vacation in fifth grade, I tried to sneak a stocking to Ezequiel. I'd hidden away some of my Halloween candy and a couple presents. Bo, by then, had learned Santa didn't exist. I guess Jason had teased him for being naive because Jason's acne, which had been clearing up, broke out in neon green zits. Millie told Mom the doctors had no explanation.

As I put Ezequiel's presents into the stocking, I found a note stuck onto a Baby Ruth wrapper with some chewed nougat.

Ha, ha. Don't you love Christmas?

The handwriting was too cramped for me to recognize it.

I gave Ezequiel the stocking anyway and waited for the demonic hordes to ascend to my bedroom. I even dreamed Abraxas, his white hair flowing, picked me up with his cape flapping like Batman's and then dropped me right into Satan's lap. But other than the usual traffic back and forth from the casino, Hell didn't seem interested in me.

But Bo hounded me. He put bubble gum everywhere in my room. I woke up with it in my hair. I got blamed for chewing it in bed, of course. He decorated Goldie's bowl with it. He gave Bobby Sherman a Bazooka mustache. And when I first got my period—enough said.

"Have you ever seen where they throw people? Kimaris took Ezequiel and me there tonight."

In the muted light, Bo's face grew pale. My stomach knotted. What had happened to my friend? What did it mean for Ezequiel to be damned without a halo?

Bo's voice did the funny squeak Jason's had been prone to lately. "He did?"

He nervously bit the fingernail of his left pinky and his tail twitched, sending one of my slippers flying. It hit me on the head.

"Ouch!" A realization hit me with full force, stronger than being whacked by the house shoe. "You're scared."

Bo picked at his cuticle. "Me? No way."

"You're afraid like a human. You're afraid of Hell as any of us are."

"Oh, *pleeeease*, do not refer to me in the same sentence as the human species." Bo rolled up the magazine and rose to his feet. "And you'd better get those tickets."

Bo slapped his hand over his mouth.

"Wait a minute. Kimaris only told me tonight he wants them. Why are you so chummy with him?"

Bo's hand stayed on my doorknob. I leaned over to Goldie and sprinkled some food in her bowl, but he didn't move.

"He's my uncle."

I dropped the container in Goldie's bowl and had to fish it out. I dried my hand on my pants. "You're joking."

"Daddy Abraxas is embarrassed he has a brother who's a goon." Bo scratched his nose. "I've always felt sorry for him."

"You're capable of feeling sorry?" I regretted my words as soon as I said them. Bo clearly had an itsy bitsy teeny weeny bit of humanity. He did care for Rhonda. But didn't he realize he was as creepy as his uncle?

The Bo I knew and didn't love emerged and shot me a dirty look. "Why would you care?"

"I don't."

"Yeah, right."

Bo slammed the door behind him.

The next morning, Mom stood in Connie's doorway with her hands on her hips, speaking only as loud as she dared so she wouldn't wake up Daddy.

"You're not wearing that to school."

I dragged myself from the bathroom, so sleepy I barely walked without running into the walls.

She glanced at me. "Charlotte, wash the toothpaste off your chin." She turned back to Connie. "Do you want me to tell your father what you've been up to, young lady? If you don't straighten out, I will, I promise you."

As I shuffled back to the bathroom, Connie shouted loud enough to wake the dead. "I dare you, Mom."

I worried about Connie too. Jason told Rhonda, and Rhonda told me, Connie had a reputation at J.F. Kennedy. I guessed neither told Millie because she would have let Mom know. To put it another way, Connie was very popular with a lot of boys, not only Freeman. She also spent every break in the girls' bathroom on the farthest corner of the school where cigarettes weren't the only things passed around.

Connie bumped into me as she stormed down the hallway. Dresses at both of our schools were supposed to be no shorter than the tips of our fingers when our arms hung down, but Connie had hiked her skirt a good three inches higher.

The front door slammed. Mom leaned against the wall, hiding her face in her hands. I walked over and wrapped my arms around her. She turned in the loop they made and placed her cheek next to mine. I stood almost as tall as she did, four foot nine and still growing, I hoped.

"Charlotte, if it weren't for you and Bo, I don't know what I'd do. Thank you for being such a good girl."

My persecution of Rhonda never registered with our mothers. I had something on Rhonda, though, which must have stopped her from tattling in her less forgiving moments.

Right then, that something emerged from his room.

Hell-boy had woken up. The wobbling hall no longer made me dizzy. I didn't know why no one else in the family noticed when our house leaned in and out of dimensions, but I'd stopped trying to figure it out.

Bo stepped out in the guise I resented the most, the baby of the family.

I'd gotten so upset once I grabbed him once by the ear and pulled him into the bathroom. "Excuse me, but I'm officially the youngest around here."

He'd wailed like a mashed cat, and I had to spend the day in my room for torturing my little brother. This morning, though, he put on the best performance ever. He waddled out in diapers with his thumb in his mouth.

Mom dropped our hug, picked him up and tickled his distended stomach. "How's my little man, my baby boy, my sweetums?"

He giggled and thumped his tail happily along the flank of her body, which she didn't register, and then put his thumb back in his mouth.

"You're a little boy who's got doo-doo in his diapers." She handed him to me. "Charlotte, be a love and change your brother while I fix breakfast."

I skipped the pancakes. On my way to the bus stop I promised I'd be kind, sincere, and a good friend to Rhonda. I'd keep my end of my bargain with Bo, despite his performance that morning. I practiced being sweet, repeating, "Good morning, Rhonda, how are you?" in my friendliest voice, thinking about what I'd learned in Sunday school the last time I'd gone to church. I was only seven, but it didn't matter. I remembered the lesson: *Do unto others...*

Bo, in his obnoxious middle school persona, had already arrived when I got to the stop and stood with his arm around Rhonda. They shared an apple fritter, seemingly lost to the world around them. As soon as Bo noticed me, he gave me a look that shouted, "Gotcha."

When I opened my mouth to greet Rhonda, my demon roared instead of the angel I'd been trying to cultivate. An unbearable itch flew from my heel to my thigh. It demanded scratching.

"Look, there's a couple tons of lard feeding on themselves."

Some of the kids laughed, but a boy with sandy blond hair whom I'd never spoken to yelled, "Cut it out, Charlotte."

He knew my name?

Rhonda broke into tears. No more stoicism laced with sugar. I finally did it. A part of my heart burned in shame, that damn conscience of mine, but the wormy part got a sick kind of satisfaction, the way it feels to pick a scab.

"Can't you leave me alone for one morning, Charlotte?"

Bull's eye.

Bo tore a chunk of the fritter and handed it to her. "Face it, Rhonda, my sister is an asshole extraordinaire."

Bo and his fancy vocabulary.

The bus pulled up, and I sullenly walked up the steps. Mr. Teddy now drove the middle school route. He'd never turned on the radio in the years I'd ridden his bus, but that day Frank Sinatra blasted away with *Strangers in the Night*.

A mustached ninth grader named George banged on his seat. "Oh, come on. Stop torturing us. Put on some rock and roll."

All the kids echoed him, "Rock and roll, rock and roll," competing with Frank's song. Mr. Teddy pumped the volume even higher, drowning their voices.

Bo planted a kiss on Rhonda's cheek.

My science test was a joke. Of course, Bo got out of taking it. He spent the period studying Mrs. Arnold's chameleon, his body as still as the animal, one reptile in communion with another.

The events of the previous night took a particular toll. I nodded off in Social Studies while Mr. Blair talked about the invasion of Czechoslovakia that had recently happened, but Bo stabbed my back with a pencil and woke me up. I tried to ignore him, but when he didn't stop, I turned in desperation.

He smiled with evil glee. "You can always count on those godless Russian Commies."

"You should know."

Mr. Blair walked up to my desk. I smelled the cigarette he smoked in the teacher's room over lunch. "Charlotte, pay attention."

I slunk in my chair and caught Rhonda eying me. Her head snapped to the front of the class. I softened a bit towards her. She did need to lose weight. I'd bullied her out of a concern for her health.

A little paper airplane flew over my head and landed on my desk. I unfolded the wings. Bo had scratched a note inside.

You're delusional, Charlotte.

Bingo!

I made the connection. Why hadn't I noticed before that Bo scribbled all over Burning Sands and Hell?

Mr. Blair asked Bo to turn off the lights, and we watched a filmstrip about the Cold War. I felt sure Daddy Abraxas, Uncle Kimaris, and probably the Great Spawn Generator—Satan himself—had to be ecstatic about the Iron Curtain.

At lunch, the cafeteria ladies played Sinatra tunes. Since my encounter with Rhonda, guilt made the paper burn so badly it caused a blister on my heel. I went into the office to get a band-aid and found the nurse humming a line from "The Lady Is a Tramp."

When I got home, Daddy hadn't left for work yet. Mom had her arms around his neck. Frank crooned "I Did It My Way" on the radio.

Mom turned her head toward me. "You'll never guess what's happened. Frank Sinatra is putting on a benefit concert for the LVPD at the Burning Sands, and your daddy has tickets.

The Jackal

Daddy didn't smoke cigars in the house, but he took an El Producto Blunt from his shirt pocket, peeled off the paper ring, threw it on the counter, and gnawed on it for a few moments. Then he took it from his mouth and pointed it at Mom.

"That goddamn Captain Hartman made a deal with Mr. Abraxas. Mr. Abraxas said the Burning Sands is a swanky joint, and we need performers like goddamn Sinatra. He told me that as a former cop for the department, I have to come for—" Daddy bit down on the cigar again and spoke through his teeth. "—good fucking relations."

Mom walked over to him and hit his chest with her fist, right where the strap to his holster would be. "Walter, that's enough!"

Daddy had never used the F word before in front of me. I went into the living room and curled up on the couch. How long would this last? Going to my room and putting my head under a pillow to block their bickering never worked. I tried how many times? Even if I played music, their voices seeped through.

I needed those tickets. I needed to endure the fight to find out where Mom would stash them.

Daddy's voice rose. "You are probably thrilled pink, aren't you, Juney? Both of your boyfriends together, Frankie and Mikey. You probably called Hartman and put the goddamn idea in his head. And here, I'm reporting to that S.O.B. again"

Mom's tears didn't mask her anger. "You have to ruin everything, don't you? You can't stand it if I'm happy."

They went back and forth for another half an hour. I remained frozen as their words hit me like bricks.

Would Daddy be grateful when the tickets disappeared? A cold sheen of sweat washed over me. Did Abraxas know about Kimaris's plan?

The door to the garage slammed. A minute later, the car's ignition turned over and then the car backed out. I sat in silence, unable to move. Mom padded in her house shoes from the kitchen to her white purse she'd left on the recliner. She sat down and put the tickets in her wallet.

She clicked her purse shut and looked at me. "I hate that man, Charlotte. I left him once. I went home to Indiana. The divorce would have been final in three weeks, but then he came and promised he'd change."

I stared at her purse.

"Your grandma told me not to go back, but I felt sorry for him. The second biggest mistake in my life. The first? Marrying Walter Jackson." Mom clutched the purse to her chest. "But if I had divorced him, you and Connie wouldn't have been born."

No mention of Bo? I checked the Christmas picture. Only Connie and I were in our pretty dresses. I wished Mom had divorced Daddy, then I wouldn't be alive to face this dilemma.

Mom walked across the room and sat next to me. "This is so unfair to you, Doll Baby. I should get you ear plugs." She squeezed my hand. "I'm going to call Millie."

She left her purse on the couch. I put my hand on the silver snap. Click, I opened it. Click, I shut it.

Click—

Connie came home a few minutes later, her foul mood from the morning lifted. She threw her books on the couch and flopped next to me.

"What's wrong?"

My sister could always read my mood.

"Daddy and Mom have tickets to see Frank Sinatra at the casino."

I lied. They were now in the back pocket of my Levis.

Connie leaned back and stared at the ceiling. "No way."

I explained how Abraxas told him he had to go.

She took my hand. "We're in for it."

I shifted, expecting my butt to hurt as much as my heel did but nothing scorched me.

Mom's footsteps came down the hall. She'd put on lipstick, brushed her hair, and exchanged her house shoes for a pair of black patent leather pumps.

"They'll be here in an hour."

Connie let go of my hand. "Who are?"

Mom picked up her purse. A river of dread almost pushed me off the couch. What if Mom wanted to show the tickets to Connie? But she only took out her compact and looked into it. She smacked her lips together a couple of times. "Millie, Rhonda, Jason, and we'll finally get to meet Mr. Nelson."

"Jason's coming? Shit, Mom."

"Shit" and "Mom" morphed into each other as Connie stretched each word. She made it halfway to her room by the time Mom finished scolding her for using that type of language in her house.

My heel began to throb. "Even Rhonda's coming?"

"Of course, and you better be a good hostess."

What did that mean?

I disappeared into my room for some private thinking time. I took out my pen and drew the fire falls I'd witnessed the night before in lava-like red. I made tortured faces and contorted arms and legs. The ink turned into oily pastels. For a moment, the bodies and the fire became animated, cascading down the paper. My hands were covered with florid hues. I didn't dare rub my eyes, so I blinked a couple of times. My picture resolved itself back into two dimensions.

I didn't understand how Hell processed dead people. Why did some burn, and why some, like Ezequiel, were put in secretarial positions? No doubt I wasn't bound for Glory, so where would I end up when I got to Hell? Maybe learning the filing trade with Ezequiel would give me an in for a cushy job.

Ezequiel's halo had turned to dust. What did that mean? My stomach felt like I'd swallowed rocks.

The doorbell rang. I sighed and put my picture down. Mom opened our front door. Amid the hellos, a man said, "Very nice to meet you, June."

"So nice to meet you too, Mr. Nelson. Girls, our guests are here."

Daddy wouldn't have liked Mom being addressed by her first name by a strange man, or any man for that matter. He didn't even like her having Millie as a friend, so she kept visits a secret.

If Daddy knew a Canadian card shark had stepped inside the house, he'd explode.

I cleaned my hands with a dirty shirt next to my bed and stepped in the hall that shimmered the way roads around Vegas did when heat blasted them in the summer.

Connie stuck her head out her door, her hair in rollers. I smelled the mist rising from the automatic curler set she'd gotten for her birthday. She mouthed a four-letter word and disappeared back into her room.

I slid along the hallway's wall forcing one foot ahead of the other. Everyone had gathered in the kitchen. Mom had pulled the sodas from the refrigerator.

Her hand hesitated for a moment. "Would you like a beer, Mr. Nelson?"

"Please use my first name. It's Hayden." He pointed to his clothes: black pants, a white shirt, and a bow tie. "I'm working tonight, but I don't drink anyway."

Mom took a deep breath. Daddy would know if one had been missing.

"It's my first night at the Burning Sands, actually. They pay double time on holidays, if you can believe that. Millie says your husband works security. I'll introduce myself, if I have a chance."

Millie and Mom exchanged a look. Millie hadn't told Hayden about how jealous Daddy got? Chances were Mom had asked her not to.

Mom handed Heydon a Verner's. He was getting the good stuff. "Oh, please don't bother. He isn't supposed to socialize with the other employees."

Hayden noticed me hanging around. He put out his hand. "And you must be the beautiful Connie, eh?"

"Charlotte." Millie, Mom, and I said my name at the same time. We laughed nervously.

Jason towered over everyone. He'd grown almost a foot in the last year. Mom had recently mentioned how relieved Millie felt that he'd lost his baby fat and hoped the same thing would happen with Rhonda. We wandered into the living room and sat down, Millie and Hayden on the couch, Jason in the recliner, and Rhonda and I sitting crossed legged on opposite sides of the room.

Mom fiddled with her fingers. Millie scooted closer to Hayden and patted the cushion next to her. "Oh, June, sit down, will you?"

Mom settled next to Millie. "What brings you to Las Vegas, Hayden?"

Hayden's stomach pooched over his belt. His hairline receded, and the arc of scalp above his forehead made his head look slightly slanted. He wore black heavy glasses, not unlike Daddy's. He didn't look like a card shark. He looked ordinary, like he taught math or worked in an insurance office.

"I've always enjoyed playing cards. I can't believe I get paid for dealing blackjack. But the weather here is what called me." He faked a shiver. "I don't like winter in Toronto."

Millie put her hand on Mom's arm. "So, you're going to see Sinatra tomorrow night?"

Despite her fight with Daddy, Mom glowed at the mention of her crush's name. "I might need to pinch myself to wake up."

Hayden crossed his legs and put his hands behind his head. "Sammy Davis, Jr. showed up at his last show in Tahoe. He's one of my tribe, you know."

Mom stared at him for a moment, and then a look of comprehension passed over her face. "You're Jewish?"

"Is the Pope Catholic?" He nudged Millie, and the adults laughed again. He pointed to his thinning blond hair. "My dad's folks came from Sweden, but my mother's a Jew."

Connie came out of hiding holding her geometry book. She looked like a water buffalo, her hair puffed and flipped up at the end.

"*This* must be the beautiful Connie."

Yep, Hayden Nelson might look like an ordinary Joe, but this guy knew how to work the ladies.

He stood up and held out his hand. Connie took it uncomfortably, leaving her wrist a little limp. She pulled away before they had a chance to shake.

She stepped over to Jason. "Would you help me with a couple of algebra problems?"

Jason's face lit up. Poor guy, lovesick with my stuck-up sister. Connie, despite her faults, took grades seriously. Even though she was using Jason, his face glowed as though they were on their way to the prom instead of our kitchen table.

Mom glanced back and forth from Rhonda to me. "Why don't you two girls visit in Charlotte's room? No need to stay with us grownups."

Up to this point, I'd been successful not having to be alone with Rhonda since my worm had chewed its way into my life.

"I like being with grownups."

No dice this time.

"Charlotte, I'm sure Rhonda would love to play Parcheesi with you."

I walked to my room on a death march. Rhonda trailed behind me. Bo's door came in and out of focus, the hallway in full tilt. I entered my room. Rhonda looked green and put a hand on my door frame to balance herself.

I pulled her inside so she could get her balance. "No one else has ever noticed the way the hall wobbles when Bo is on his way back."

Rhonda no longer looked seasick, but didn't she hear what I said?

"I love your curtains. Are they new?"

"I've had them for two years." Had it been that long since we'd been alone together? My heel smarted, and I suddenly felt weepy. Her saying something nice irritated me more than if she'd punched me in the eye.

Ok, I'd be a good friend. I'd make one last attempt to straighten her out. "How can you stand to be with Bo?"

Rhonda had a ready answer. "Are you a nincompoop? Bo treats me better than you do."

"You're the only one he's ever nice to."

Not quite true. Bo would run and get Daddy a beer anytime Daddy wanted one. And there were the times when Bo appeared as a toddler the two of them snuggled on the couch for those wrestling matches.

"Bo's redeemable." Rhonda said this as though her belief was fact. "Isn't that what makes you trust Ezequiel, believing he'll get out of Hell one day?"

Goldie's little face watched us. She made little fishy kisses on the side of her bowl. I focused on my fish as I considered what Rhonda had said. I didn't think Ezequiel belonged in Hell, but his being able to escape never crossed my mind. Rhonda attended church regularly and probably had knowledge about redemption. I didn't want to shoot myself in the foot by arguing.

I collapsed in my inflatable chair. She pushed my journal away and reclined on her side on the floor, resting her head in her hand.

I frowned. "Bo's already lost. You know what his real name is?"

"Behemoth." She was such a know-it-all. "God created Bo as a wild beast, and that's why he has a tail. But the Bible doesn't tell Bo's full story. He slowly developed a soul because that's what happens if you live for eons unless you are entirely despicable. But then he found out God planned for him to be eaten by humans when the world ends. It's laid out in the Book of Job. So, Satan promised him if he became a demon, he'd have a family and wouldn't have to worry. Abraxas adopted him, but Bo had been so traumatized he ~~kept~~ became addicted to junk food, and—"

Rhonda sat up and glowered at me with a raised fist.

"Bo knows what it's like to be teased. When I get to Heaven, I'm going to have it out with God, and he better pay attention to me." She put her hand down. "Charlotte, I know about your trips to the filing room."

An invisible faucet like the ones that filled the glasses with Coke in Purgatory opened over my head. Shame rushed through me. If I had drawn my shame, it would have been the color pink, pink and pulpy and indigestible.

"I'm not going to Heaven."

Rhonda scooted closer to me. "Of course, you are. Everything will work out. All will be well, even for a meanie like you. But I am worried about you."

I looked over her head and gazed at Bobby Sherman. She didn't know the things I'd imagined doing with him. "I wish I had your confidence."

Rhonda turned her head to follow my gaze. "You don't have any friends, unless you count Jason."

"I'm not Jason's friend."

She turned back toward me. "Then why is he the only person on the planet you confide in?"

He was?

Oh, God, he was. Ezequiel technically wasn't on Planet Earth by right.

Jason and I'd gotten in a habit of talking to each other on the way home from school almost every day. He rode his bike beside me as I walked from the bus stop, and we both knew he went out of his way. Every afternoon we'd commiserate with each other in his hopeless quest over Connie and our mutual dislike of Bo. I'd gotten in the habit of looking forward to it, though after I dropped a thousand hints about Bo, Jason never caught on.

Rhonda snapped me out of my reverie. "Bo is the only person I've ever met who accepts me," she slapped her thighs, "just the way I am."

Okay, my turn to share a hard truth. "Bo's poisoning you with sugar and fat."

Rhonda's lips went white. My heel stopped burning. I kept needling. "This morning Mom asked me to change your boyfriend's diapers, so forgive me if I can't see in him the wonderful things you do."

Rhonda only knew the boy who'd grown up with us since fourth grade. "You've lost it." She looked down at the picture of Hell I'd drawn and picked it up. "What's this?"

"Hell. I went there last night."

I needed a hug. Rhonda probably did too, but my sock burned as though it had been stuffed with embers. My heart grew darker, and I got a wonderfully terrible idea.

"Let's check out Bo's room the way we did Jason's."

In the years Bo lived with us, I never found the courage to cross the hall and open his door. But if we explored it together, Rhonda might wake up about her boyfriend. I'd be doing her another favor.

The worm took another nibble from my heart. I told myself the pain felt good, like sucking on your lip after you'd bitten it.

"Does Jason still have the picture of Connie in with his socks?"

She shook her head. "He only has a little one in his billfold now."

"You really want to go to Bo's room?"

Rhonda didn't need a second. "Of course, I do."

We tiptoed into the hall. Hayden's voice drifted to us. "Kids today have so much more to deal with than we did. That LSD, for example—"

Mom interrupted him. "Isn't it awful? Those hippies frighten me so."

The floor rippled in waves.

Rhonda put her hand on Bo's door and her mouth next to my ear. "Last year when they tested the H bomb, our floor moved like this."

I placed my hand on the knob. A mild jolt of electricity hummed through my skin, but I held on and twisted. The door opened with a soft pop.

Rhonda grabbed my shoulders and yanked me back before I stepped inside. "I've changed my mind."

"He's been your boyfriend for how long now?"

I left her in the hall.

The room was too neat for any twelve-year-old boy to inhabit. "Nothing's scary in here."

Rhonda followed me in and closed the door behind her. "Looks like your mom cleaned."

"Mom's never been here. If Bo isn't in the house with one of us, this room doesn't exist."

Wouldn't a real boy have sports pennants, pictures of motorcycles, or rock bands, and dirty clothes strewn across the floor? The walls were bare, painted the institutional green of the hallways of Dwight Eisenhower Junior High, and the room empty except for the bed and dresser.

He didn't have a closet to Hell?

Rhonda sat on Bo's bed and bounced on the bedspread a couple of times while I tried to open the top drawer of the dresser. It wouldn't budge. Rhonda came over to help me pull. No luck. We tried the other drawers, but they were locked too.

Rhonda spied a skeleton key hanging on the wall above the dresser.

"Here we go."

She grabbed it. I stepped back, and she put it into the lock of the top drawer. First, she pushed it in upside down. And then she dropped it. I reached over impatiently to rip it from her hand, but she finally slipped it in.

"Charlotte, something's happening."

Fear shredded her voice.

The dresser began to shake. Streams of multi-colored light came out of the lock and reflected off Rhonda's peaches-and-cream complexion until she shone with a deep purple hue. Then a spectrum of color flashed through her like a revolving rainbow. Rhonda's hair stood on end, and she shook like she was having a seizure. A flash filled the room, and for one terrible moment, her skeleton glowed cartoon-like through her skin.

I grabbed Rhonda's waist and tried to tug her backwards, but an electrical current throbbed through her body into mine. My teeth rattled against each other while the rest of me turned to jelly. I felt my bones melt.

A giant slurping sound engulfed us, and our bodies turned into light as we were sucked into the drawer. On the other side, we became flesh and blood again. I fell hard on top of Rhonda, my chin hitting her shoulder.

"Oh, that hurt."

I tasted blood and rolled off Rhonda, who lay unconscious. I leaned over to see if she was breathing. To my relief, her chest rose and fell. I shook her as the stream of light that delivered us faded.

Would our families realize we'd disappeared? Maybe they'd forget about us the way everyone did with Bo, and we'd be stuck forever in this stupid nowheresville of a drawer.

My knees sunk down in something mucky, like swampy ground. The possibility of quicksand terrified me.

"Bo? I know you have to be close by." The pulse of dripping water spread through the silence. I curled next to Rhonda's body. "Rhonda?"

She groaned. "I hit my head."

I gazed upward. A patch of light streamed through the keyhole. like an angel with outspread wings. I helped her sit up and pointed. "We've fallen at least thirty feet."

Rhonda leaned against me. "What should we do?"

The water kept a steady beat.

"Maybe we should try to find where the water's coming from. Can you stand?"

She groaned. "I think so."

We clung to one another, making our way through the gloom. The air enveloped us, thick with humidity. Soggy ground sucked at our shoes.

Rhonda breathed heavily. "I'd take Vegas at 110 degrees any day over this. I think the ground's firmer here."

She stomped to shake off the muck covering her sneakers.

"Don't. Someone might hear us." I grabbed her elbow. "Come on."

We took three more steps, and then our feet splashed into boiling hot water. Screaming at the top of our lungs, we jumped out.

Rhonda screamed at the top of her lungs.

"I hate you, Charlotte Jackson. Do you have any idea how badly you hurt my feelings day after day after day? I've tried to turn the other cheek, but look what you've gotten me into. I'm in Hell, for goodness sake."

She crumpled to the ground. I collapsed next to her.

"Goodness has nothing to do with being here, Rhonda McAuley, and it's about time you understood."

My words had no effect on her.

"Everybody hates you. No one wants to be around you. You're a bully, and the other girls despise you because of the way you treat me."

The truth of her words sank in. I'd never been invited to a slumber party. No one ever came to my house. When Daddy was sure not to be home, Connie had friends over, music and laughter would percolate from behind her closed bedroom door. I'd stopped asking other girls to visit because they always had excuses not to come. No wonder I hung out with Jason.

An image of a jackal formed in my brain with teeth bared. She moved in a predatory circle.

You don't deserve to have friends. You're an outcast as I am.

My second demon had been born.

Revelations

The horrible things I'd said or done to Rhonda took the shape of my jackal. The beast circled, haunting me. One memory after another flashed through my mind as she hissed her accusations.

You're no good.

"I'm sorry for the way I've acted toward you. I'm so sorry for the things I've said."

I reached over to Rhonda, but she batted away my arm.

"Too late, Charlotte."

An eerie glow surrounded us, as though Rhonda's words lit a torch. I stared at murky, roiling water, too ashamed to turn my head in her direction.

A pop echoed on the other side of the pool, Bo squeezed through an arch almost hidden by steam. "Rhonda, are you alright?"

Tottering towards us, he grasped an extra-large Coke in one hand and a submarine sandwich in the other. Stepping out of the boiling water, he ignored me and offered Rhonda the soda. She grabbed it with both hands and drained half the bottle.

The jackal's breath burned my neck. *You don't deserve to ease your thirst.*

I lowered my head.

Bo took a bite from the sandwich and chewed for what seemed like forever. After half a millennium, he swallowed. "Follow me, and don't say a word."

Rhonda and I hesitated at the edge of the pool.

Bo took her hand. "The water won't burn you if you hold on to me."

Rhonda stepped in.

I wanted to trust someone as much as she trusted him. I wanted Ezequiel to find me, but Hell existed in a universe of its own. And I forgot to bring the match to get us home.

I stood zombie-like at the edge. Bo gave the sandwich to Rhonda and thrust out his other hand. "You too, Charlotte."

We crossed, the water's temperature now more like a hot bath. On the other side, Bo wedged himself through the arch and disappeared, but his voice carried as clearly as if he stood before us. "Come on through. One at a time."

Rhonda slid through the arch, which now began to look a bit like a McDonald's sign. The dimension must have been stretched like a balloon blown past its capacity.

POP!

Bo comforted Rhonda in a low, soothing voice.

"Each drawer in the dresser leads to someplace different, but this is my favorite. It's my private burrow. No one else knows about it. I found it a few months after coming to Earth."

Had they forgotten I stood on the other side of whatever divide the arch created? The pool generated immense heat again. The back of my Levis were being ironed against my legs.

Strangely, the one place on my backside I didn't feel would ignite was the heel of my sneaker.

I counted to three and walked into the arch. Darkness surrounded me for a second, then a large farting noise accompanied me into Bo's hidey hole.

Rhonda's eyebrows crossed at the stench. "Charlotte, you should be ashamed of yourself."

My jackal, my ghost-shadow, followed with her lips pulled back, mimicking the curl of Bo's mouth as he watched me appear. Greasy wrappers from hamburgers and candy bars scattered over the dingy carpet. In the mix lay a few copies of *Boy's Life*, some pulp science fiction, and several issues of *Seventeen*.

On the cover of one of the *Seventeens*, a young woman with a daisy in her dark hair wore a somewhat conservative two piece swimsuit. I picked it up and pointed to a headline: "Who Would Go Out With a Girl Like Me?"

"Discover any good dating tips, Bo?"

Bo snatched the magazine from my hands. "The fiction section happens to be excellent."

He gathered the other reading material and stacked it neatly on a desk behind a mattress flung on the floor. Three different sizes of calligraphy pens, the tips all perfectly aligned in a row, a pot of ink, a stack of cream colored paper, and the same type of pen Ezequiel had given me were laid out so tidily their belonging to Demon Boy seemed miraculous. A black book, possibly a journal, rested in the seat of an office chair.

Bo grabbed a pair of briefs hanging over a lampshade and shoved them beneath the covers of the mattress. I collapsed on it, trying not to think what else might be under me. I closed my eyes and eavesdropped on my former best friend and my demon brother.

"Charlotte talked me into checking out your room. Bo, I wanted to see where you lived."

A long silence hugged the air. They were kissing. I turned in embarrassment to face the wall.

Bo came up for air. "I'll get you out, don't worry, but you have to wait here for a while. I have an errand to run. Whatever you do, don't leave."

I fell into a long empty sleep, waking to Rhonda sobbing.

She sat at the desk reading the black book. She cocked her head. I pushed myself off the mattress and walked over. The book turned out to be a journal. Bo's elegant script covered the pages.

I've succeeded in increasing Rhonda McCauley's natural inclination toward gluttony and am happy to report she has gained fifty pounds in the years I've been assigned to this mission. Please note her friendship with Charlotte Jackson has been adversely affected due to my interference.

Rhonda glared at me. "Go ahead, Charlotte. Say I told you so."

The jackal snarled. *You've hurt your friend for years, your very best friend.*

I took a step back. "I'm not going to do that."

"Just as well I found this." Rhonda threw the journal to the floor. "I'm hideous, aren't I?"

"No, you are so pretty. Your skin is perfect. And your hair. I've always wanted hair like yours."

"Stop it, Charlotte. I'm sick to death hearing about my damn complexion. I know what it means. People are trying not to say I'm a fat monstrosity."

Rhonda stood and crossed her arms. I copied her gesture, tongue-tied, unable to explain the spell I'd been under. The jackal laughed without remorse. Another wave of shame swept over me.

Rhonda didn't seem to care if I said anything or not. "I'll show him. And you. I'll show everyone. I'll lose this weight. I'll only eat lettuce leaves, if I have to."

I felt like a rabbit caught in a snare. I wanted to go back to sleep and fall into blackness for a long, long time, and when I did wake up to be far from the hells in my life: my family's, the mess I'd made with Rhonda, having no friends, and the real Hell I stood in.

"Do you still think Bo's redeemable?"

Rhonda misinterpreted the intent of my question. "Stop teasing me."

"I'm not. I want to know."

She didn't answer and picked up a *Seventeen* and stared at the cover. "I hate perfect girls."

I whispered a familiar prayer. *JesusMaryGod*. But it felt useless. If a God, or Jesus, or some Mother in the sky who came down to appear on screen doors to give people comfort were real, they'd have to be satisfied with the only thing I had to offer, my desperation.

The darkness folded in on itself, a black hole in space. But then, a pinpoint of light appeared on the wall above the desk, tiny and perfect, like the first star at night. I blinked, and it vanished. I did my best to pray for it back, but God didn't care. I only stared into nothingness.

Footsteps echoed through the tunnel. Rhonda put down the magazine. We froze like statues. I sensed her holding her breath as I held mine until Bo's familiar grunting reached our ears.

He squeezed through the door.

"Coast is clear. I tell you, Hell has emptied out, but the Old Guy still has a few patrols loyal to him. Let's go."

I expected Rhonda to leap into a full-frontal attack and call him every name in the book, but she followed Bo and me in silence as we twisted and turned through tunnels. Two male demons dressed in Nehru jackets and paisley bell bottoms hurried past us, carrying suitcases. The shorter of the two, barely taller than me, led a chihuahua with the tiniest little horns on a glittery leash. The dog nipped at my ankles.

Bo kicked it away and let them know who was in charge. "The Sands doesn't have a pet policy, you know."

The chihuahua whined. Chartreuse wings sprouted from his back until he resembled a miniature doggy dragon. He flew into the arms of the smallest demon who gave the finger to Bo.

"Can it, Shorty."

Like he had any room to call names.

We turned left, left again, and then right, entering the hallway full of eyes and ears. I knew where we were. I ran down the corridor to Room 777 and tried the doorknob. It stayed still as a rock. I searched for the spare key, but it had disappeared from the niche.

I banged on the door. "Ezequiel. Let me in."

It screeched opened. I faced Kimaris who towered over a very nervous young woman.

Her lips slowly formed, "Help me."

Kimaris clamped an oozing hand on her shoulder. He looked truly happy to see me. "Well, well, what do ya knows, it's the little girlie friend." He unfolded the long fingers of his other hand one by one. "Gives me them tickets."

No way. As soon as I got home, I was going to slip them back into Mom's purse.

"Where's Ezequiel?"

Bo and Rhonda caught up to me.

Bo leaned one hand against the wall to catch his breath, right on top of an eye. The ears around it grew red and wiggled as though they were suffocating.

"Charlotte, I left you and Rhonda to see if the gossip about Ezequiel is true. And it is."

I didn't think Rhonda would have a thing to say to Bo, but she'd been drawn in. "Gossip?"

Bo nodded. "He's been promoted to full-fledged demon."

Kimaris grabbed my shoulders and spun me around. He reached into my back pocket and pulled out the tickets. "I knews you wouldn't disappoints me, girlie friend."

He twirled me around to face him, picked me up and stared straight at me. Kimaris didn't bother to control the slime leaching from his fingers the way he did when he played cards with Daddy. My shoulders were getting soaked.

"Angel Boy's halo didn't fools me one bit. I knews it was only a matter of time his sensitivity and poutings and feelings sorry of himselfs would turns into old fashioned evil."

He dropped me, and I toppled into Rhonda who'd inched closer to us.

Kimaris again clasped the shoulder of the young woman. What had she done on Earth to make her believe she deserved to serve time in the filing room? He slammed the door in our faces.

I turned to Bo. "Ezequiel had at least another fifty years as an underling. He told me so himself."

Bo shrugged. "Labor shortage. Look, I've got to get the two of you back."

I didn't want to go home. Not without the concert tickets. But what choice did I have?

Bo led us back to the platform under my bedroom closet. He pulled a match from behind his right ear and scratched it on an empty crate. Rhonda moaned with fear as we flew upward. Lucky for her we didn't have to take the alternative route through the ground itself the way I had on my first visit. She'd probably have had a heart attack.

Bo led us out of my closet. The grown-ups were laughing again in the living room.

Bo held out his hand. "Which one of you has the key to the dresser?"

Rhonda pulled the key from the waistband of her pants and threw it at him. "I'm an assignment? You were using me."

The blood drained from Bo's face, if demon anatomy consisted of blood. "Daddy Abraxas made me do it. He made me come and said I had to be mean, so I tried and wrote down what I knew he wanted to read. But after I met you, I wanted to make you happy and share the junk food I love. Everything is Charlotte's fault anyway. She didn't file your paper. Instead she stole it and brought it to Earth."

Rhonda focused on the last thing he said. "What paper?"

I slipped off my shoe and looked inside as Bo explained about the filing policies of the Netherworld. Rhonda's day had turned to ash. I turned it upside down and flakes floated to my bedroom floor. The jackal licked them up.

Mom's voice came from the hall. "And this is Charlotte's room."

She opened the door. As Hayden and Millie followed her in, Bo and Rhonda slipped out.

Millie made a pleasing little gasp. "I love how those blue curtains contrast the peach paint. June, you should think about going into interior decorating."

"Well, I've been trying to convince Walter to knock out the wall between the kitchen and living room to open things up."

Hayden gave a big toothy grin. "What a fabulous idea, June."

My heart hurt. She had no idea what was in store with Daddy when he discovered she didn't have the tickets.

The jackal sat on her haunches and scratched her side with a hind leg.

To my horror, the pictures I'd drawn lay on my bed face up. Mom spied them. "Charlotte, be a little more careful. You'll get pastels on your spread."

Maybe I'd shrivel up and disappear down the hole in my closet for good. She picked them up but didn't focus on the images. I let out my breath.

But Hayden paid attention. "Wait a minute here. Can I have a looksee?"

Mom finally processed my tour de force. "Charlotte, what were you thinking?" Her voice trembled. "Why can't you draw horses and flowers like you used to."

You'd think I drew naked people instead of lost souls screaming in desperation as their tortured bodies writhed in unimaginable pain.

Hayden took the drawing from her, studied it for a long moment, and then gazed at me, his Mr. Goodtime mood erased from his face. He held up the paper and pointed to a detail of a man's terrified face I'd sketched in the bottom left corner.

"These drawings are very original. Charlotte. You're quite talented."

Mom put her hand to her mouth. "I can't imagine why you'd draw such things."

A soft whistle escaped through Hayden's teeth. "June, whatever you do, don't discourage her. I used to teach art. For her age, Charlotte's compositions are very advanced."

I became legs and arms, ashamed of having my secrets scrutinized, knowing how uncomfortable Mom felt. And yet, Hayden said I had talent.

The jackal pulled back her teeth. *He's a liar. He's only trying to charm you.*

Millie leaned over and peered at the pictures. "You were an art teacher?"

"For fifteen years. I decided to try a completely new life after my third marriage didn't work out. Drawing and playing cards have always been my passion. I make more money dealing cards than teaching. I owe a lot of alimony."

At least Hayden was an honest scumbag.

He put the picture on my desk. Mom finished the tour, ignoring Bo's room. Everyone then assembled in the kitchen where Connie, Jason, and Bo were drinking Coke floats. Rhonda leaned against the counter next to the cookie jar, gripping the edge on either side of her, her knuckles turning white.

Hayden looked at his watch. "Time to go. I'll drop you all back at the house and then go to work."

Mom walked outside with our guests to say her goodbyes.

Connie sucked on her straw and slurped the last of the ice cream. "I'm going to ace the next test." She placed her glass in the sink and then bent down to stare at her reflection on the side of the toaster. "What do you think of the hair?"

I lied. "Looks great. Doesn't it, Bo?"

Bo held a scoop of ice cream, refilling his glass. "Definitely."

The front door slammed. Mom strode into the kitchen, her body shaking. "Charlotte, I've never been more embarrassed. Why on Earth would you draw those disgusting pictures?"

Connie ran off toward my room. "I'm going to have to check these out."

I shouted at her back. "Don't look at them." Alone with Mom and Bo, I tried to defend myself. "Hayden said I had talent."

My jackal rubbed her coarse hair against my leg. *He was only being nice.*

Mom's voice echoed my new demon's tone. "Throw those pictures away. They're sickening."

Bo squashed ice cream almost to the rim. He stayed quiet for once. I wanted to cry, but my tears had been taken by the fire the night before.

The jackal's whisper became sandpaper scraping the inside of my ears. *Shame on you. Now you've hurt your mother.*

Connie walked back in. "Charlotte, these are good." She giggled. "You're wicked."

Mom grabbed my drawings out of Connie's hand, wadded them into a ball and threw them into the trash. She walked out without another word. Connie skipped two steps and pulled them out. Placing them next to her math homework, she smoothed out the wrinkles.

"You're not a lost cause, after all. Can I have these?"

I shrugged.

Connie smiled. "I'll keep them safe. If you want to draw anything you want to hide, I've got places where I stash stuff."

I turned to Bo. "I suppose you'll rat on us."

He'd eaten enough of the ice cream to pour some Coke into the glass. "Me?"

His tail looked as slimy as ever, but something was off about him.

Connie gave me a kiss and headed to the door. "I'm going out for a little while."

My sister escaped to whatever private places she had.

I rinsed one of the glasses. Putting it on the dish rack, I realized the difference in Bo.

"Where are your horns?"

Bo reached reflexively for his head. "I have no idea."

I instinctively knew Bo told the truth. This time, at least.

That Old Black Magic

Around six o'clock the next evening, Bo, Daddy, and I sat at the kitchen table as Daddy cleaned his service revolver. Simon and Garfunkel's voices floated from Connie's room, filling the house with the fifteenth rendition of "Mrs. Robinson."

Bo slumped in his chair. His hand kept reaching to his head. Mom, her hair in curlers and wearing a housecoat over her slip, put a tray of fish sticks into the oven and turned on the timer. She hadn't said another word about my tortured bodies.

My stomach was heavy like I'd swallowed the bullets Daddy had pulled from his gun. I could have exploded from the inside out. Before Mom started dinner, my heart stopped as she transferred her wallet, lipstick, and keys from her everyday beige purse to her black handbag with the rhinestones. She never took the tickets out to look at them, so I didn't have a complete heart attack.

But what would happen when they got to the casino, and she didn't have them? Would Daddy be able to bluff their way into the concert since he worked there? Would he ever let her forget she'd lost them?

Daddy reached for the tumbler he'd half filled with whiskey and took a sip. "Goddamn Frank Sinatra."

Mom turned from the oven and fixated on his drink as she chewed her bottom lip.

Daddy gave the cylinder a whirl. "I can't believe I have to listen to that S.O.B. singing in person. Bad enough the bastard's records play in the office all day long."

One by one, Daddy replaced the bullets and snapped the cylinder back into place. Mom tossed tomatoes and cucumber into the bowl of lettuce and then touched Bo's forehead.

"Are you okay, son? We shouldn't go tonight if you're getting sick."

I felt one bullet lighter.

But Bo perked up and smiled. When did he get braces? Mine were due to be put on in a week. He was such a copycat.

"I'm fine, Mommy. It's important you don't miss the concert."

Mommy? I eyed him. Neither of us called her Mommy anymore, at least when he manifested as a preteen.

Daddy took another drink and put his gun in his holster. The jackal walked from the living room like a ghost, baring her teeth in a hungry smile, then turned and went back the way she came. I did my best to look normal, but pins and needles spread over me. I gripped the table's edge to keep from falling apart.

Bo pushed out his lower lip. He reached for the glass, moving it away from Daddy's arm as though to make more room. "Would you like to play Chinese Checkers?"

Whiskey had molded Daddy's eyelids so they drooped. The muscles around his mouth slackened. He pushed his chair back, ignoring Bo. "I have to put on that goddamn suit."

Daddy got up, picked up his glass and disappeared down the hall.

The timer dinged. Mom pulled out the tray and clicked off the oven. "I guess I should get dressed too. At least we have a ride to the casino tonight." She let out a big sigh. "I wish we never got those tickets. I'm on pins and needles."

The condition seemed to be contagious.

After Bo and I filled our plates. Connie materialized out of her room the first time since noon, her fingernails painted pale blue. She'd spread eyeshadow up to her eyebrows in the same shade. Her dark roots showed above the water buffalo hair-do.

Bo and I picked at our food. Connie harpooned a fish stick with her fork and held it up. "This stuff's awful for my complexion." She put half of it in her mouth. "Don't either one of you dare to tell Mom or Daddy, but I'm not babysitting tonight. I'm going out with Freeman."

The three bites of Mrs. Paul's I'd managed to swallow churned in my stomach. A worried look must have plastered my face.

Connie picked up another piece with her fingers. "Don't be such a worrywart, Charlotte. I'll be home before they get back."

Daddy walked back into the kitchen in his dark blue suit and the one necktie he owned decorated with blue and gray diagonal stripes. In private, Mom joked alcohol had pickled Daddy because he didn't look his age, considering he should be up for retirement in a few years. He filled the tumbler again. To me, he looked like Robert Mitchum, who also seemed to be pickled in the movies.

Mom followed him out a couple minutes later. She used Loving Care on her hair, and she'd combed it out so soft dark waves spread back from her forehead, falling to her shoulders. She wore a black dress that had hung in her closet forever and a pair of shiny black high heels I'd never seen. She must have borrowed them from Millie. They wore the same size.

"Connie, can you help me with the zipper?"

Connie got up, chewing the last bite of a fish stick.

Mom put her hands on her belly like the women did in the five pounds slimmer commercials. Connie maneuvered around Daddy who glared at Mom. I imagined the scene at the entrance to the casino's theater. Mom searching in her wallet, shaking her head, maybe apologizing, and Daddy screaming at her so loudly Frank backstage was sure to hear.

Connie ran her hands under the faucet and then dried them. Mom turned her back to Daddy so Connie could reach the zipper.

"Breathe in, Mom."

The doorbell rang. A low voice called from outside. "Las Vegas Limousine Service."

Daddy set his glass down with a clink. "Don't know why we needed a jackass to drive us. Limousine service, for Christsake."

Mom had her handbag over her arm by then. "Walter, Mr. Abraxas is showing you how much he appreciates having a former policeman as head of security. This night is to honor you."

Daddy took a handkerchief from his pants pocket. He blew on his glasses and started to polish them. I smelled his breath from where I sat.

Bo scooted back in his chair. He walked up to Daddy and put his hand on his jacket where the gun lay underneath. "You don't need to take this."

I inhaled an inch deep. What was Bo up to?

Daddy ignored Bo for a second time. He strode to the door and opened it. His shadow and the chauffeur's passed across the curtain in the kitchen window.

Mommy gave each of us quick kisses on our foreheads. She smiled. Her makeup cracked a bit. "Don't give your big sister any grief, you two."

Her heels tapped on the floor until the living room carpet silenced them. The front door closed. Her shadow appeared behind the curtain and she was gone.

Connie immediately called Freeman. Ten minutes later he honked his horn, and she whisked herself from the house.

I turned on the TV, dropped into the couch and nibbled a hangnail. Nothing to do but wait until my parents got home, but after a few minutes I realized Bo was doing the dishes.

I checked on him to make sure my senses weren't deceiving me. "Bo, are you feeling okay?"

He'd put on one of Mom's aprons and was scrubbing the tray.

He shook his head vigorously. "I don't think so, Charlotte. I couldn't help myself. I had to tidy up." He reached for a towel and dried the tray. "I've been having strange feelings since last night."

I took the towel from him and started on the glasses he'd placed in the dish rack. "Delayed puberty by 5,000 years?"

"Not those types of feelings." Bo touched his heart. "I'm feeling soft here. And it aches. I'm worried about Daddy, and—"

I didn't know this creature who was washing the silverware, "And what?"

"My tail hurts."

We both looked at it. The skin had faded to a sickly shade of gray.

I gave him my best diagnosis. "It looks dehydrated, Bo."

Without thinking, I touched his forehead like Mom had done. His skin felt warm but in a normal human sort of way.

Bo cleaned the countertops. I left him to his new obsession and slunk back to the couch, afraid my jackal would jump out of the television set. I sensed her watching me. We'd bought a new painting at an art sale in the mall the week before, and it now hung above my head. A woman in a long white dress sat beneath a bent cypress tree looking out at an unsettled sea. Would she transform into my jackal and lunge into the living room?

Or would the jackal show up as a fourth head in the Easter picture?

I pulled my legs up, trying to make myself as little as possible, waiting for the jackal, waiting for monsters. I imagined Mom panicking as she searched through her handbag, and Daddy's face growing red as he humiliated her in front of the policemen waiting in line behind them. He yanked her by the arm to the parking lot where he didn't have his car, screaming at her in the backseat of a taxi the whole way home. When they got here, finding Connie gone, the rest of the night became a hellscape.

The sky darkened outside the sliding glass door. I whispered a feeling I never allowed myself to admit. *I wish Daddy would die.*

I reached for the lamp, but Bo got there before me and switched it on.

He eased himself next to me and turned off the TV. "They're on their way."

My bedroom door opened. Kamiris and Lily walked into the living room. Kimaris wore a dark blue sergeant's uniform, neatly pressed like Daddy's suit. I glanced at his feet. He had enormous shoes fit for Bozo the Clown.

Lilith chewed gum noisily, her dark hair ratted and pinned haphazardly to her head. She wore a low-cut evening dress sparkling in gold glitter with a slit to her left thigh.

"Oh, the human is here."

Lilith's hips swung from side to side as she glided over to me. I watched the spikes in her high heels make indentations in the carpet. She'd been playing me before with her visits? Was her appearance at the screen door the first step in a long-term plan to see Sinatra? I couldn't fathom why she'd act like a floozy and date Kimaris.

Lily leaned over me, her breasts in my face. They were frightening. For dear life, I didn't want to ever have more than B cups.

She whispered loud enough for Bo and Kimaris to hear. "I need to powder my nose. Can you show me to the little girl's room?"

She caught my eyes with a look of desperation.

I slipped off the couch. She followed me back down the hall, but pulled me into my room instead of the bathroom.

"I'm sorry, Charlotte, but I'm breaking out of Hell for good tonight. I had no idea Kimaris planned to involve you." She reached into her cleavage and drew out my parent's tickets. "I told him I loved Frank so much I needed a little of him next to my—"

I expected her to say heart. But did she have one? Did Bo? I looked at the tickets as though they were dipped in poison. What good would they do for me now?

She didn't complete the sentence. "I've been working on this for centuries, but I never thought I'd pull it off. Mary's been coaching me. She finally talked the On-High to give me a dispensation. Can you believe it? But I can't be anywhere near Hell to make it work."

Kimaris started to belt out the lyrics to *That Old Black Magic* from the kitchen. Lily took my hand and placed the tickets in it.

I closed my fingers over them. "Lily, I don't understand. Isn't the Burning Sands as bad as Hell?"

"If Abraxas has his way, it'll be worse. As long as I don't step inside, I'll be okay. Look, sweetie, you and Bo are going to the casino with us. You catch up with your mom and give these to her."

Kimaris's voice bellowed. "Hey, Lily, how much powder can your nose hold?"

I had on the same pair of Levis as the night before. I put the tickets in my front pocket this time.

"I don't understand."

Lily spoke quickly. "When we get there, I'll make a run for it. I got some help." She pointed upward. "Kimaris will be confused, and you can find your mom. You'll be with Bo, so they'll let you in."

"Your prayers are being answered?"

Lily smiled, but then blinked back tears. "Well, there are stipulations. But at least I'll be free." She smacked her gum and stuck her head outside my door. "Coming, Sugar."

When we returned, Bo was pouring Kimaris whiskey into the tumbler Daddy had used. "Daddy Abraxas says I'm doing a real good job up here, Uncle K."

"Makes sures I don't hears any different."

Kamiris straightened his tie and snapped his fingers. The doorbell rang, and he motioned for me to answer it. A middle-aged man in a crew cut wearing a uniform more elegant than any police officer's stood ramrod straight.

"Las Vegas Limousine Service."

This guy had an English accent. Kimaris must have paid extra. He offered Lily his arm.

"My dear, let's us be off."

She took out her gum and put it underneath the end table where the lamp rested. "Okay, honey, let's find out what the big deal is with this champagne I've heard about. Oh, by the way, the kids are coming with us."

Bo's head shot up. "We are?"

"Theys are?"

Lily's perfume hung in the air like a spell. "Didn't Abraxas tell you? He wants his son to see Sinatra tonight, and he told me to bring the girl along."

In the limo, Bo and I sat on a wide cushy seat across from Kimaris and Lily. Neon lights flashed by my window like psychedelic sideshows. I'd only seen the Strip on TV commercials. Daddy had never taken us there. Imagine that. I'd turned twelve and lived in Las Vegas my entire life.

When Daddy had been a cop, my family went to Fremont Street on occasion. Mom and Daddy would take turns standing in front of the casinos with Connie and me while the other went in to gamble. Mom only played the slots and would be back in half an hour. Daddy took longer, but we had fun nonetheless surrounded by pulsing neon and watching Vegas Vic wiggle the cigarette in his mouth and wave his arm.

Connie and I tried to guess how soon he'd say, *Howdy Partner*, again, counting down 10, 9, 8...for about a hundred times before he did so. I remembered when I realized the sign said *Pardner*, not Partner, and felt smug I caught on before Connie did. Other than these visits, my experience of big-time gambling in Vegas were the stories Daddy told about work and the one arm bandits in the supermarkets.

The driver turned onto Las Vegas Boulevard. Bo scooted over to me, squishing me against the window. He pointed to the *Welcome to Fabulous Las Vegas* sign.

"Did you know the Strip is four and a half miles outside the city limits."

I stored the piece of trivia in my mind to dazzle Connie with, but decided she probably already knew the Strip was bogus Las Vegas.

Lily reversed the cross of her legs. Kimaris put his hand on her thigh. She smacked it.

"Not so fast, Sugar. First Frank, and then I'll give you my complete attention."

Kimaris groaned in a way that made me push myself further into the seat. We passed the construction site of a new casino to be called Circus Circus. A rumor at school circulated that a carnival for kids would be included. We passed the Flamingo, the Tropicana, the Sahara, and other places where Daddy said the mob raked in the dough and from where unfortunate gamblers took long drives into the desert.

Finally, the Burning Sands towered to our right. We turned, slowing down behind a line of other limos and inched our way through two huge signs. On both sides FRANK SINATRA rose ten-foot high in Bo's penmanship, flashing neon-red, neon-orange, through the neon spectrum, and then replaced by a ten-foot Old Blue Eyes in a tux, and back again to his name.

I elbowed Bo hard in the side. "Really? They recruited you to do this?"

Bo backed away a few inches. "Daddy Abraxas says my handwriting is the one thing I'm good for."

"Bo?"

"What?"

I jutted my chin out so he'd look behind him. My skin crawled with the heebies jeebies. His tail had fallen off and lay on the seat like a dead snake had disconnected from his bottom.

We edged our way through the giant Franks. Kimaris leaned over Lily and stared out the window on her side. Fountains of flames shot from marble walls lining the drive. They morphed into ten-thousand-dollar bills, and then into columns of anti-gravity lava reaching so far that the top of the limo blocked us from seeing how high they actually went.

He whistled. "Abraxas outdid himself tonight."

The back of his arm pressed against Lily's breast. She scrunched her face in disgust, lifted her left leg and jabbed her high heel into a Bozo shoe.

Kimaris yelped in pain, pulled himself back, and raised his hand as though to slap her.

But she'd prepared herself. She'd taken off her gloves. She pointed her index finger, it's nail manicured and trimmed but pointy enough to take out an eye for eternity. Her body glowed so her skin melded with the golden fabric of her dress. An aura of light surrounded her, bright enough for Bo's tail to sizzle and turn to ash.

"I am Lilitu, demon born of Sumer, born of the Oldest Order. I am the agent of sacrifice. I am the one who refused to lie beneath Adam or beneath any man. I am the one who created Hell with my past partner Satan, known as Ba'al, known as Asmodius, known as Applyon, now known as the Old Guy."

Bo and I took each other's hands and squeezed tight. The limo parked in the portico. The promotions claimed the entrance had been carved out of a solid block of the largest ruby ever found. I didn't believe rubies got so big, but maybe they found it in Texas.

"I denounce Hell. I denounce who I grew into being. I reclaim my soul to the On-High. I confess to wreaking havoc for millennia and in more dimensions than your lowly status doesn't have the imagination for. I have repented for over two thousand years. I cast off the last shred of the demon who lived within me, with whom I have wrestled. I finally conquer it at this moment."

The limo door opened. Lily's aura dimmed, but a stronger, warmer light washed in. A woman, who looked like Lily's sister, poked her head in and smiled.

"Ready, Lily?"

She extended her hand.

"Ready, Mary."

Lily took it and stepped over Kimaris's big feet. He appeared frozen in place. Only his lips moved, repeating foul words over and over.

Bo pulled me out as well. Mary and Lily let go of their hands. Lily's body shuddered. Black fur grew over her and she shrank into a cat. She ran off, back down the long entrance toward the real City of Las Vegas.

I held onto Bo's arm for dear life as Mary guided us off the portico to the front of the gilded doors festooned with Bo's script: *Burning Sands Casino.*

Mary didn't bother to glance inside. "Bo, the On-High sends apologies. You weren't supposed to be eaten at the end of the world. There was a problem with the translation."

Bo's body trembled.

Mary put her hand on my shoulder. For a second, everything went dark except for an echo of the pinpoint of light I'd seen in Hell the night before. But then I snapped and became aware of the hustle around me. Cops disappeared through the casino's doors, one by one, in their dress uniforms and shoes so polished the red light of the portico reflected in them.

Mary kissed my cheek and put her mouth close to my ear. "Be brave, Charlotte. All will be well, but life on this plane sucks a lot of the time."

She dematerialized.

Bo and I turned to each other and spoke in tandem. "We have to find Mommy!"

Kimaris had unfrozen and now watched us from inside. His shoe had sprung a leak and oozy yellow liquid sprouted like a baby geyser. A guard opened one of the glass doors for us but put out his hand to stop us from going any further.

Uncle K squishy-stepped up and slipped him a bill. "He's Abraxas's kid."

We were waved through, but Kimaris grabbed us both by the arm.

Bo stared at his uncle. "Where's Mommy June?"

"Your mother is by the slots nears the bar, right in fronts of the theater. You're goings to haves the time of your lives."

He let go as though we were pieces of trash. I didn't have time to ask how he knew Mom's location.

Had Daddy found out about the tickets? Were we too late? Bo pulled me along, but then stopped and pointed to a huge clock spanned the ceiling. The minute hand ticked like a heartbeat through the jangly music of the slots.

We had ten minutes before Frank's show would begin.

We ran. I said a thank you prayer because Bo knew where to go. We wove around the demons in the Nehru jackets who must have left the chihuahua in their room.

And there she was. Mom sat on a stool next to a slot machine, the contents of her purse on her lap. Her head moved side to side as if she were thinking, *No, no, no.*

Her purse dropped to the floor. "What are you two doing here?"

I pulled out the tickets.

Bo provided our cover. "We found them on the kitchen floor. We took a taxi here." The bar's entrance opened to our right. He glanced quickly at it and then back at us.

She grabbed the tickets. "Daddy should be coming out any second. Bless you two, but where's Connie?"

My jackal sauntered out of the bar and sat on her haunches. Hayden and Captain Hartman followed her, involved in a conversation. They stopped a few feet in front of us.

Hayden glanced around, but we were invisible to him. "I came to find you, Captain, because I knew you'd want to know. This is only my second night working here, but Mr. Abraxas already wants me to play shenanigans with the customers, like he knows about my former life. I gave it up fifteen years ago. Twelve Steps, you know."

Captain Hartman took notes. "I'll see to this first thing tomorrow. I already have reports that things aren't what they should be around here."

The lights dimmed and the whirly noises stopped. A woman's sultry voice broadcast through the room. "Last call for seating."

The lights flashed back on. Daddy stepped from the bar, unsteady on his feet. The booze had worked its way through him.

Hayden saw him and smiled. "Hey, Mr. Jackson, I've been wanting to meet you. I've been sharing some things with Captain Hartman here, I think you may already know about. By the way, I had the pleasure of getting to know your wife last night."

Mommy squeezed my shoulders so hard I knew she needed me to hold herself up.

Daddy screamed over the casino's noise. "You sons of bitches. Both of you." His head whipped to us. He fixated on Mommy. "You might as well fuck both of them here and now."

He pulled out his gun and pointed it to his head. I squeezed my eyes shut a half second before the shot blocked the hypnotic music of the slots. Gunpowder burned my nostrils. Screams pierced my ears, aftershocks to the blast.

Arms surrounded me, yanking me back into the aisle of slots by several feet.

"Don't look, Charlotte."

A familiar voice. Hands grasped my arms.

"Look at me. Look at me and nowhere else."

Bo's cries of "Daddy, Daddy" lanced the screams of the casino's patrons. I tried to turn around, but Ezequiel caught my head. He had grown older in spirit. In body he was still a teenage boy, but his bearing held a darker intelligence. He no longer wore his leather jacket. No more Little Joe Cartwright hair. It hung to his shoulders now. Daddy would have called him a goddamn hippie. His black suit looked expensive, as did his white shirt with ruby cufflinks and his thin red necktie. His horns were resplendent now, cast in gold.

"I'm here to get him. Do you understand?"

I shook my head, unable to talk.

"I'll take care of him for you. I promise."

He vanished into thin air just like Mary did.

Abraxas's smooth voice came from somewhere behind me. "We were going to relieve him of his duties after tonight."

Captain Hartman gave a curt answer. "Is that so?"

The jackal prowled around me with soft footfalls. My face imprinted upon her face, her canine teeth, my teeth, her claws, my fingernails.

You got what you wished for. He's dead.

I brought my arm to my mouth and bit until it hurt.

Once A Cop

The blast of the gunshot continued to ring through me, reverberating with the blinking lights and buzzing that announced a woman's jackpot farther down the aisle. My jackal circled at my feet as I turned to see Captain Hartman holding Mom. Her knees almost touched the floor. Her dress hiked up as he maneuvered her back to the stool, an ungainly dance in blood splattered clothes. The tickets lay on the carpet inches from a growing red pool.

Shouting and shrieking filled Burning Sands, but Bo's screams underlined the bedlam's score. A blonde woman in a floral evening gown now knelt at Mom's side.

Captain Hartman put a hand out. "Don't move, Charlotte." He took two long strides toward me. I stared at the stains on his shirt and pants. "My wife's with your mother. We'll get your family home."

He drove us in his own car. Gabby Hartman sat in the back seat where Mom curled next to her repeating, "Your daddy is dead, Your daddy's dead." In the front seat between Bo and Captain Hartman, my left arm touched the fabric of his uniform, my right against Bo's soft flesh. Bo stared straight ahead, his hands gripping his thighs.

Millie waited for us on the curb. The TV news must have already reported what happened. Several neighbors, some in their robes, had gathered around her.

Captain Hartman stepped out first. "Go back to your houses and give the family privacy."

Slowly, alone, in pairs, they wandered to their homes, glancing back from time to time before they disappeared inside.

Freeman's Mustang turned the corner and slammed to a stop in the middle of the street.

Connie jumped out. "It's true? The radio said Daddy was shot at the concert."

She flew into Mom's arms. Bo and I held on to one another until something brushed against our legs.

Bo bent down and scooped up a black cat. "I guess Lily wants to live with us."

⫸⫸⫷ ⫷⫷⫷

The mail came early the day of Daddy's funeral. We found an envelope with a return address from Palm Springs tucked in with the telephone bill and the ad for Market Basket.

On the couch, Connie and I sat on either side of Mom as she opened it. Mom drew in her breath. "It's a condolence card from Frank Sinatra. *So sorry for the loss of your husband and father.* He actually signed it."

Connie put her head on Mom's shoulder. "That's pretty nice considering Daddy ruined his concert."

Bo slumped down in the recliner with Lily curled in his lap, his face mottled by tears. I glanced at the Easter picture. Bo, now a cuddly toddler with a big smile and pudgy knees, sat between Connie and me in our yellow dresses. He wore a little seersucker suit and clutched a blue bunny the same color as his outfit, a normal baby boy not sticking out his tongue or trying to squeeze the life out of a real rabbit.

Daddy's brown shoes lay next to the recliner in the living room. In the bedroom, his shirts and pants hung next to Mom's clothes. The change he jangled nervously in his pocket was strewn across the top of their dresser next to a couple El Producto Blunts in their wrapper.

The whiskey bottle remained on the counter of the kitchen. No one had touched it.

Tap-tap. No one had locked the front door. It opened, and Millie called in a soft voice, "We're here."

Mom refused the funeral parlor's limousine. She said she never wanted to see a limo again. Hayden drove us to the cemetery. Millie followed in her car with Jason and Rhonda.

A rare winter rain tapped on the canopy above where we sat. Daddy's coffin was a metallic gray green, the same color as the Caprice he'd bought only six months earlier. Did Mom pick the color on purpose?

Grandma in Indiana wasn't well enough to fly to Las Vegas, but she had never visited anyway. I sat between Connie and Rhonda, who held my hand. Hayden, Millie, and Jason filled the first row of seats. Captain Hartman and his wife took chairs behind Mom's. Mark and Chuck, the two patrolmen who played poker with Daddy from time to time were next to them.

Bo stood between Mom and the poles of the canopy with his hands folded in front of him, shifting from one foot to another, focused on Daddy's coffin.

My jackal ran next to the car as we traveled to the graveyard. She now lay in front of Bo, panting. Her hungry eyes didn't leave my face.

Hayden and Millie had helped Mom arrange things like getting the preacher from the Baptist church and an old woman from the choir to sing. Her white head reached Pastor Bob's shoulder, but she held a large black umbrella high enough to cover both of them as he spoke about eternal life. Daddy had been a good father, a good husband, a good cop, a good head of security, and someday we would understand the mystery of God's mercy.

The preacher concluded with a prayer. *World without end. Amen. Amen.* He walked under the canopy, almost stepping on the jackal's tail.

The old woman lowered the umbrella and began to sing.

I come to the garden alone
While the dew is still on the roses
And the voice I hear falling on my ear
The Son of God discloses

The song flowed like waves over us. Mom, Connie, and I melted into our grief. My heart broke open and warm tears soaked my face.

And He walks with me
And He talks with me

The jackal's head snapped up.

Rhonda gasped and squeezed my hand. "Charlotte, there." She bent her head in the direction the cars were parked. "Do you see them?"

I'd slept with Mom since Daddy died, afraid he'd be escorted by Kimaris through my room and down the long shaft to Hell where Ezequiel would wait for him. I only went in there to feed

Goldie, but my shoes remained in place on my closet floor. I touched the wood once. It felt cool to my fingertips.

Now at the edge of the lawn, Ezequiel and my father watched the service. Ezequiel wore the same fine suit he had on at the casino. Daddy was dressed in his sergeant's uniform, the one he wore when he didn't work undercover. He held his hat in his right hand. The rain slicked down his hair and splattered his glasses.

And He tells me I am his own.

"Daddy!"

Everyone turned to look at Bo except for Rhonda and me. The singer's voice quivered as it grew louder.

And the joy we share as we tarry there

None other has ever known

The preacher tried to comfort him. "There, there, son."

A black limo turned into the cemetery drive. The song continued, but the words seemed farther and farther away. Rhonda's grip tightened. The limo parked behind Hayden's car. Kimaris got out of the driver's side. He now wore the uniform of the police commissioner. He walked around the limo and opened the back door.

Abraxas climbed out in the same get-up he wore the first time we met: the black Zorro cape draped over his shoulders and his long white hair flowing free. He walked next to Ezequiel and put his hand on his shoulder.

My jackal languidly strolled in front of me, turning her head, and bared her teeth.

Your fault.

She loped over the graves and leaped into the back of the limo. Abraxas scanned the mourners. His rubies irises caught the sun and flashed, and then a scowl scissored across his face. Bo moaned.

Daddy raised his free hand. *I love you, Charlotte.*

He told me this. I swear he did.

Abraxas reentered the limo. Daddy followed him. Ezequiel remained for a moment longer. Rhonda put her arm around my shoulders.

I also swear Ezequiel put his hand on his heart, and his voice carried over the graves. *I love you, too, Charlotte.*

⋙⟫ ⟪⋘

The McCauleys and Hayden came for dinner that evening. At dessert time, Connie and Jason went into the living room to watch the Smothers Brothers. Bo quietly disappeared into his room. Rhonda and I sat with the grownups at the table.

Hayden pressed his fork to pick up the last crumbs of chocolate crust from his plate.

"Captain Hartman resigned as soon as this Kimaris fellow replaced the commissioner. No one knows where he came from, some city down south somewhere." He sucked on his fork for a second. "Anyway, June, it looks like your husband was figuring things out and working with the LVPD."

The circles under Mom's eyes were almost black. She'd been getting in and out of bed through the night, every night, shuffling around the house, turning on the TV, turning it off. Or she lay next to me worrying about how to pay the bills, or about Daddy being cold on the slab in the mortuary, and about the awful moment when the undertaker told her Daddy had to have a closed casket.

Mom sipped her coffee, leaving a lipstick ring on the rim. "Walter always said, once a cop, always a cop, but I didn't believe him. I never thought he'd be willing to work with Captain Hartman again, especially—" She looked out the window. "Since he was so troubled and believed that the two of us were—"

We gave Mom time to compose herself.

"Hayden, I'm so ashamed of what Walter accused you and Captain Hartman of doing."

Hayden pushed his plate away. "I've had my share of troubles with the law, but I grew to respect most of the officers who dealt with me. If Mr. Jackson hadn't had his breakdown, I'm sure things would have been cleaned up. Now, the Burning Sands will have the department in its back pocket."

Rhonda hadn't touched her dessert.

I'd never seen her do that before. "You're not going to eat it? It's from Marie Callender."

She looked away. "I'm not hungry."

Hayden took his plate to the sink. He picked up the whiskey bottle. "Charlotte, is the rubbish can in the garage?"

"Yeah."

He went out the door with it and returned empty-handed.

I doubted Hayden's news. Daddy had idolized Abraxas, but did his cop values take the upper hand when he saw the vice going down at the casino? I tried to calculate the odds Hayden told us this to make Mom feel better. They had to be more than 50 percent. Isn't that what people did for the dead? Made up stories glossing over what they were really like?

On the other hand, the paper Ezequiel had pulled from the cart in Hell describing Hayden's character told the truth about him, but it no longer mattered. Millie told Mom he admitted to being a slimeball for a long time.

Was Daddy driven to desperation because he believed the man he had to work with was fooling around with Mom?

And Hayden? He just said an innocent thing about meeting Mom at the worst possible time.

I shuddered.

Millie got up and poured another cup from the percolator. "Okay, I'm going to change this dreadful conversation. I have an announcement. I am going to be the first woman to ever sell cars at the dealership."

Hayden took her hand when she sat down again. "Sign of the times, June. Wives have almost as much to say about big purchases as their husbands."

Millie nodded and smiled. "You'd do my job with your eyes closed. Starting on Saturday, I'm giving you your first driving lesson." Mom's face blanched, but Millie scooted her chair an inch closer to her. "You're not going to say no. I'll be here at ten o'clock sharp."

I grabbed Rhonda's neglected plate and walked to Bo's room, a permanent fixture since Daddy's death.

He'd left his door open a crack. I knocked with my free hand. "I got some pie for you, Bo. Can I come in?"

I took his grunt for a yes. The room already resembled his nook in Hell. His clothes were everywhere. Copies of *Seventeens* and his school books lay in a pile at the bottom of his unmade bed. He'd propped himself with pillows, reading my copy of *Earth Abides* he pilfered from my room.

Bo's blue bedspread had a design of baseballs and bats, though he never expressed any interest in sports. I tugged at it and made a place to sit, handing him the plate.

He took a bite. And then another.

I watched Bo eat. He finally put the plate on the floor next to a Baby Ruth wrapper. He smelled the way an eleven-year-old boy should smell, not pleasant. Maybe Hayden would talk to him about hygiene.

Bo went to his dresser. "I've got something to show you."

He opened the top drawer. No jolts of cosmic juice flew out, so I joined him. Only pairs of white socks lay in the drawer. I remembered how Rhonda and I sneaked into Jason's and discovered Connie's picture. Maybe Bo hid a few of Rhonda's beneath the pile before me.

And then it hit me. "You can't go back to Hell?"

Bo shoved the drawer closed. "I'm banished. I hate being human. It hurts too much."

I didn't try to console him. "My Hell door has closed too." I wanted to find Ezequiel. "Bo Ezequiel would never turn evil, even escape the filing room. He said he'd make sure Daddy would be okay. What did he mean?"

Bo kicked a pair of pants out of the way, revealing his teddy, a stuffed bear without personality. He picked up the teddy and held it to his chest. "Uncle K told me Ezequiel's in management now, in charge of the whole database. He won't let Daddy Walter fry unless there's a really good reason, but you can't trust him anymore, Charlotte."

A horn honked outside.

"I won't be too late," echoed down the hall.

How dare Connie take off, tonight of all nights.

"Is there any way we can get down there to find out more?"

"Charlotte, do you know what would happen to me if Daddy Abraxas knew I came back to Hell?"

"What would he do?"

"Oh, come on. Use your imagination. I've done the worst crime any demon has ever committed. I learned about love. Forget about Ezequiel, Charlotte. He can't let himself care about you anymore. He's a demon now."

"He said he loved me at the funeral. I know he did."

"Forget about Ezequiel." Bo flung his teddy against the wall. "There is no way for us to go back to Hell. Both of our entry points are sealed. We have to live our lives."

"Bo? Charlotte? Come and say good night."

Bo picked up the bear. "Be there in a sec, Mom." He placed it on his pillow. "Do you think Rhonda will always hate me?"

I assumed he asked me, not his bear. "No, I don't. Come on, Rhonda deserves a goodbye from both of us."

Hayden was helping Millie into her coat when we rejoined everyone, but he looked at Mom. "Hey, don't worry too much about Connie. She's at that age."

Hayden didn't know much about Connie. She'd been *at that age* for a long time. Poor Jason, he couldn't even get her to watch an entire episode of the Smothers Brothers with him.

We started to walk out to the cars. Rhonda pulled both Bo and me back and let the others go ahead. "Bo, did you see the demons and Mr. Jackson?"

My brother nodded.

Millie waited in front of the Fairlane. "Time to go, Rhonda."

"I'm coming." Rhonda turned back to us. "So, why did Ezequiel have wings?"

All Shook Up: 1971

Abraxas wrung exactly what he wanted out of Daddy's suicide. The news stations called his death a scandal. With so many police at Burning Sands, someone should have been able to intervene. Innocent people were traumatized. How many others would have been killed if he had turned the gun on the crowd?

Within a few weeks, good cops followed Captain Hartman and resigned or were forced out by threats and blackmail. A report on the local news even featured "the blue exodus" as houses were put on the market all over town and former LVPD officers found jobs in places like Laguna Beach and Vermont. Abraxas, with Kimaris now the head of the department, manipulated the force.

Everyone in the city knew a change had come down. Whispers at school surrounded me. I was THAT girl whose Dad was THAT cop. It didn't matter Daddy had no longer officially worked as a policeman. It only mattered that he'd blown out his brains. Everyone had an uncle or an older brother who'd been there and no longer wore his blue uniform with pride.

Abraxas gained control of all of the casinos, those on the Strip, the working man's casinos on Fremont Street, and the creepy storefront ones Hayden confessed he frequented on trips to Vegas before he hit bottom. TV and newspapers sang Abraxas's praises. Mobsters had hightailed it back to Atlantic City and Miami because of his exemplary business practices and instituting such clean operations at the Burning Sands. Their nefarious ways sealed their fate. In fact, Abraxas's name was being tossed around as a good candidate for governor.

I didn't want to imagine what Hell on Earth did to scare those wise guys, but it had to be more than the threat of meat grinders and a one way car trip into the desert. Though I'm sure those methods were in the bag of tricks of the goons Abraxas employed.

As long as my family was left alone, I didn't care. The hole in my closet remained sealed. My jackal hadn't returned. Our lives were normal except for a goldfish who was 300 in human years, a brother who'd been a character in the Old Testament, and a ex-Sumerian demon, now a black cat demanding to be let out every night. We didn't need cosmic battles of good versus evil to complicate things and let what happened on the Strip stay on the Strip.

The Bobby Sherman poster was history. My cheeks grew warm whenever I remembered my adolescent crush. Now, sketches of Ezequiel covered my walls, pinned on top of each other. There might have been a hundred of them.

Mom still believed I drew Little Joe. I overheard her mention to Connie how it comforted her that I hadn't started liking real boys.

Connie had a different opinion. "Mom, this *Bonanza* thing of hers is messed up."

Thank. You. Big. Sister.

I poured my sore heart into each drawing using the pen that never ran out of ink, though now it only offered four boring colors: black, blue, red and green. The softest aquas or boldest purples streaming to my paper was a thing of the past.

I love you, Charlotte.

Ezequiel told me this in my imagination at least ten thousand times since Daddy's funeral.

I had no doubt Rhonda had seen Ezequiel's wings. Her sensibility for perceiving the impossible good in what appeared warped and maligned had been proven with Bo. She told me light had laced inside the webbing of his wings as he stood across the graves of strangers.

I did my best to imagine what they must have looked like and pretended Ezequiel never went into the black limo where my father's spirit waited with Abraxas. In my daydreams, Ezequiel's wings held the secrets to everything good that had existed in the world but had been lost. When he kissed me, his wings folded around my body, and then I'd lose myself.

My fantasies as a young teen were pure cotton candy. I knew the mechanics of sex, of course, but in my feathery world, making love with Ezequiel meant floating on a multicolored cloud. We wouldn't really "do it," only enough to feel really tingly. We'd wait for the real thing until we got married. I didn't want any miraculous conception I'd have to explain away. I didn't want to be like Connie and have a reputation. I didn't want a real human boyfriend, or a life more complicated than it needed to be.

But I did want Ezequiel to come back to me and be my boyfriend. No one would have to know. Well, nobody except for Rhonda and Bo.

On Labor Day, Connie and Freeman went to Elvis's afternoon show at the Hilton. Freeman's horn honked, and Connie sailed out of the house in a pink mini dress and gold sandals. She was going to see ELVIS, the most important day of her life, though it was too bad Freeman hadn't got tickets for the evening show.

Mom came home that afternoon with a run in her pantyhose, a red face from a hot flash, a briefcase full of work, and not in any mood to make dinner. The 1972 models were arriving at the dealership. The inventory paperwork piled on, plus the finance details from an uptick in sales of the '71s. No one at the dealership got Labor Day off with the Blow Out Clearance, when there would be even more files to process.

So, Bo started a salad. I turned on the oven for the frozen pizza that had been taking up space in the freezer when Connie stormed in the house, sobbing hysterically.

"Freeman broke up with me. We hadn't even left the parking lot after the concert. His parents don't want him to date me anymore."

Mom's face lost all of its softness. She started ranting in a way I never heard her do before.

"You don't need Freeman, Connie. I want you to date a nice boy, and he certainly isn't one. And, by the way, I want you to wear bras all the time. Why can't you go to the University of Nevada like Jason? For Heaven's sake, you've graduated fifth in your class. At least go to secretarial school."

Mom didn't want Connie to smoke dope, or dress like a hippie, or swear. Connie needed to at least get a job to help pay for things because Mom's feet were killing her, and she had a splitting headache.

Connie stood in the kitchen dripping tears. Bo threw the forks he'd tossed the salad with into the sink and left the kitchen.

I put the pizza in the oven thinking I'd follow him, but Mom kicked off her shoes and sent them flying in my path.

"I've had enough with you, Connie."

I assumed Connie would apologize. Was she blind to the lines of exhaustion in Mom's face and at least pretend to clean up her potty mouth?

Instead, my sister made fists and hit her thighs. "I hate you, Mother. I am eighteen years-old. It's none of your fucking business what I do with my life."

Connie ran out of the house like she'd done so many times before, with Mom shouting behind her like she always did. "Come back right now, young lady."

The next morning, birds woke me with their annoying songs, Dread pressed me into the sheets. Since Daddy died, no demons or goons had ventured through my room, but my panic rose second by second. I reminded myself that I'd met the Mother of God. It was a brief encounter, but it had to be worth something.

Heaven had to be as real as Hell. My parents simply bought the wrong track house. Maybe a pantry led to the Pearly Gates in another home in our neighborhood, and some other girl or boy lucked out with the visitors they received.

I forced myself out of bed. I sprinkled Goldie's food into her bowl. On my way to the kitchen, I peeked in Connie's room. She hadn't come home.

I found Bo making sandwiches. He'd grown taller than Connie, weighed at least 100 pounds less, at the edge of the oldest I'd ever seen him in his permutations as the demon boy. Now that he'd become mortal, would he continue to mature? If he did, he'd grow up with perfect teeth. His braces were off. I never got mine because Mom said they'd be too expensive for what she brought in.

On the counter, he'd lined up slices of Roman Meal bread, mayonnaise, a tomato, an avocado, and horrible things called sprouts.

I grabbed a package of Instant Breakfast and put pop tarts in the toaster. "Rhonda won't eat that."

He sliced open the avocado. "And you're going to get diabetes."

Lily scratched at the front door. I opened it and picked her up. "Where do you go at night?"

I'd asked her the same question at least a hundred times. Did I expect her to start talking? At least Lily left Goldie alone, although she did lay with her nose next to the bowl to watch her swim. Sometimes Goldie put her little fish lips on the glass and they kissed.

Above the rooftop of our neighbor's house, the intense blue of the sky warned the coming day would be a scorcher. A gray VW Bug slowed to a stop in front of the house. I closed the door and peeked through the Venetian blinds in the kitchen window.

A tall man just on the other side of being too old for Connie got out and pulled the front seat forward. Mom had made Bo and me promise to never ride in Beetles because they were death traps. She probably tried with Connie, too, but there she was climbing out of one in the mini dress and sandals.

The man's hair hung nearly as long as Connie's, reaching far past his shoulders, a dark contrast to Connie's bleached locks. He didn't look like the nice boy Mom hoped she would meet. He glanced toward the house.

Though the air conditioner had been on low all night, sweat dampened my body.

The man counted out money into Connie's open palm. She gave him a kiss on his cheek. Before I stepped from the blind, I caught a glimpse of another young woman with red hair in the back seat, and a dark-skinned girl in front in the passenger side who might have been my age.

Hoping I had a fever, I found the thermometer in my bathroom. I leaned against the sink's counter, waiting for the mercury to rise.

Connie must have eased the front door open because she startled me. "If you tell Mom I just got in, I promise you'll regret it."

Mom's shower turned on. Connie's hazel eyes were cloudy and sunken.

I took the thermometer out of my mouth. No fever, but I felt sick. "Why did that guy give you money?"

Connie's lips turned into a half smile. She waved four bills with Cousin Andrew in my face. "I went to this great party last night. I got a job modeling. This is an advance."

She went into her bedroom.

Back in the kitchen the toaster had spit out the Pop Tarts, but now they weren't hot anymore. I pushed the lever down again, poured milk into the glass and mixed in the Instant Breakfast.

Bo stirred eggs in a bowl. "You should tell Mom about Connie."

"What do you mean *I* should?"

He put a couple slices of awful wheat bread into the toaster after my Pop Tarts were done and didn't answer.

Mom came in without having brushed her hair. She hadn't dyed it in weeks, and she looked skunk-like. I doubted she slept much. She kissed my check. I now stood almost as tall as she was, all five foot two of me.

Bo finished the eggs and set down the wooden spoon he'd been stirring them with. "Got your breakfast, Mom."

Mom had on her black polyester slacks. Her shoes lay where they'd landed the night before. She slipped them on.

"Do I smell coffee? Did you kids make it for me already?"

I wouldn't take credit. "Bo did."

Mom poured herself a cup. Bo finished scraping the eggs onto a plate and buttered the toast.

Mom faced a long day ahead of her. She hadn't opened her briefcase, the work she'd brought home unfinished. She had enough on her mind and didn't need to know Connie got home riding in a death machine driven by someone who gave me the willies.

Connie towered over me at five foot six, but models were supposed to be taller, at least five nine, right? Mom didn't need to know Connie said she had a job. I couldn't imagine she'd land a gig.

Mom took Bo's hand and kissed it. "I feel like I'm on *Queen For a Day*."

⤜⤜⤜ ⥆⥆⥆

Jason had a nine o'clock class at the university. Kennedy was on the way, so we didn't have to take the bus on our first day of school. Millie had passed down her car to him. A Fairlane, owned by a middle aged woman for nine years, won the prize for the most uncool ride in the history of the high school. Since Rhonda, Bo, and I had been the most uncool freshmen the previous year, the car suited us. The odds changing our status as sophomores were pretty much nil.

But, hey, we were also the only three students at Kennedy who'd ever gone to Hell. Not invited to parties? Not an issue. We made our own fun.

Jason now wore glasses. The pale blond hair covering the line of his jaw up to his sideburns belied the fact he had no real beard yet.

He glanced back at me in the rearview mirror. "Charlotte, is your mom still only making right hand turns? Must take her an hour to get to the dealership."

"Longer sometimes. She doesn't want to turn left into the parking lot because Sahara Avenue is so busy."

Rhonda shifted in her seatbelt and looked at me. Her chin jutted in a severe point. Her beautiful peaches and cream complexion had paled, and her once luxurious hair hung thin and straight. She'd been pulling it back into a limp ponytail accentuating her too well defined cheekbones.

"You should be proud of her, Charlotte. She's managed to keep the house. You know she's never gotten over her terror about driving, but she gets in that Caprice every single day and goes to work."

Jason turned his blinker on and changed lanes. "You sound more like Mom every day."

We stopped at a light. A patrol car pulled up to our right with a driver way too handsome to be truly human. He tapped a ruby ring on the steering wheel. He glanced at our car. Bo put his elbow on the armrest and shielded his face with this hand. Being the ex-son of Mr. Sin City himself, repercussions for becoming human terrified him as much as Las Vegas traffic did Mom. Years had passed, yes, but Bo's long tenure of being the beast-child Behemoth wouldn't be forgotten.

When the light turned, the patrolman gunned his car and sped away. Bo let out an audible sigh.

Jason turned into the parking lot at Kennedy and parked at the curb. The whole way to school I'd been convincing myself

Connie would be alright, but a new wave of apprehension washed over me.

"There's something I have to say before we get out." I explained about the man and the other girls in the Volkswagen and his giving Connie money. "She says she's got a modeling job."

Bo slammed his book closed without even dog-earring the page. "I told you that you should have told Mom this morning."

Rhonda unsnapped her seatbelt. "Connie isn't tall enough to be a model."

Jason hit the steering wheel with both of his hands. "Damn it, Charlotte, don't you know what that means?"

Rhonda looked at me and then at her brother. "What *does* it mean, Jason? You want to fill Charlotte and me in?"

Jason blinked tears away. "You two can't be so stupid. It isn't possible."

Rhonda talked about becoming a nun, so I gave her credit for not putting two and two together. Me, the daughter of a vice cop? I should have known better.

"Connie's turning tricks?"

The new vice principal whose name I didn't know walked up to the car with his hands waving. Why did vice principals have such thick necks?

"Move the car now."

"Asshole." Jason gunned the car, and we peeled away from the curb. "We're going to talk some sense into Connie."

Rhonda held the dashboard. "We're going to be late, Jason. Stop the car and let us out."

He slammed on his breaks. A horn blasted through the back window of the Fairlane. Parents and students stopped in their tracks and stared.

"Get out." Jason's face turned crimson. "All of you."

Rhonda complied, but Bo and I didn't budge. Bo rolled down his window and held out the lunch he'd made.

Rhonda took the bag, looking stricken. "Thanks, but I don't think I'll be hungry."

Jason sped out of the parking lot.

We'd been gone less than a half an hour. I went to my room, hoping Connie would be there, rifling through my stuff like she did every so often. But I only found a note with the picture of Hell that had upset Mom with some pictures of Ezequiel I'd drawn.

These are my favorites. Don't stop drawing, whatever you do. Thanks for not ratting on me. Connie

I hid the note underneath my pillow, wondering if it would burn me the way Rhonda's paper had done.

Jason got on the phone and called Millie at work. My tongue felt thick, and my brain was on the fritz. Mom would be home in twenty minutes. I'd have to face her, and how would I survive?

Millie's new Mustang pulled in the driveway. Car doors slammed. Bo, Jason, and I sat in a line on the couch. I held my hands between my knees, curled my lips over my teeth and pressed down on them.

Mom spit fire as soon as she walked in. "Why didn't you tell me Connie came home so late? What were you thinking, Charlotte? Didn't you consider as Connie's mother I had the right to know what was going on with her?" Her voice broke and then rose into a crescendo. "You were the one I trusted."

Bo, human now, still had a dark side. "It wasn't late, it was early. Connie came home just before you woke up. I told Charlotte she should tell you."

A defense coated my tongue. *You were so tired. I would have told you tonight*, but anything I said would sound like justifications. Mom, Bo, and Jason would all counter me.

My last defense stopped at my lips. *Connie made me promise.*

Did she? No, she didn't make me, she had threatened me.

I finally looked at Mom. Her head had become the jackal's. My second demon had come back.

The image faded quickly. Mom looked beaten. She sank into the recliner. Its size enveloped her. Funny, how she never used it. She rarely stopped moving at home. Cleaning. Cooking. Fretting.

She stared across the room at me and then put her hands over her face. I barely heard what she said. "We can't call the police."

Millie knelt by her. "We'll figure out something."

Jason pushed himself off the couch, took three long strides to the sliding glass door and gazed at the backyard. "I'll find Connie, I promise."

His pledge sounded like a boy's. Dear faithful Jason, so ungainly and so earnest. I wanted to believe him, but how could he unearth Connie in this huge city?

Jason, Bo, and Mom went out to search anyway. Millie drove back to work, but she must have called Hayden from there. He phoned our house about an hour later and said he'd snoop around in the casinos for leads.

I thanked him and hung up. Lily had been curled on the couch for her afternoon siesta, but she now scratched at the front door, hours earlier than normal. I let her out.

Left on my own, I wanted to create chaos. I needed to destroy something. I changed to my Minnie Mouse tee shirt and an old pair of cut-offs, then jumped up and down on my bed in a fury to make it collapse.

No luck.

I spied the magic pen Ezequiel gave me. I clicked the black lever. I'd obliterate all of his faces and then rip each picture from the wall. Then I'd scribble over my entire room to make it match the way I felt inside.

How dare Ezequiel come to me when I was a child. How dare he say he loved me. He caused all of this. Daddy's death. Connie's disappearance. He used me as much as Bo did Rhonda. Free Will existed even in Hell. He should have been brave enough to tell Abraxas that he wouldn't intrude on the life of an innocent fourth grader.

I prayed he'd molder in the mailroom for even longer than eternity and held the pen to the first picture in my reach. The force of my stroke cut across the paper, but no ink came out. I tried each of the colors. None of them worked. My pen had come to the end of its life.

Behind me, my closet door squeaked along its tracks.

Go-Go Boots

Heat migrated across the carpet, climbed the bed, warmed my feet and then traveled up my legs. I put my hand on my chest to catch my breath. The fist of anger clenched inside my stomach relaxed. The best kind of butterflies fluttered up and down my spine.

If Hell had breached open, it had to mean Ezequiel knew I needed him. He must have been checking on me, and now he'd come back.

A thud landed behind me.

"Ezequiel?"

I made a slow half circle. A go-go boot lay on its side between the bed and my closet. Another sailed through the door and thumped next to my desk.

Long fingers grasped my floor. "Hates to disappoint, little girlie." Kimaris pulled himself over the edge with a grunt. "I hads to climb the whole way up. The service elevator shut down in '69."

I collapsed. My legs barely had enough strength to push me toward the wall.

Kimaris wore a bright green Hawaiian shirt decorated with gold koi and a pair of yellow and green checkered Bermuda shorts. Flip-flops were on his feet with the thong sticking between two toes the color of slug-slime-white and a mass of four outer toes, the nails on his right foot painted pastel pink.

"Geez, it's my day off. I'm havings a pedicure and drinkings a martini by the pool, when this little goon rushes out of the hotel callings, *Special Delivery for Commissioner Kamiris.* I thoughts, Oh, brother, some shenanigans is goings on and Abraxas wants me to takes care of it personal like. Last week, I founds a bunch of Hari Krishnas dancings in the fountains. I sents them straight to Naraka."

His feet slurped themselves to my desk chair. He pulled it out and plopped down. "But, nooooooos. The message ain'ts from Abraxas, but the Old Guy himselfs. I do a little works down below in case the power dynamic switches again. Beens known to happen."

"Get to the point, would you?"

"Well, ain'ts you got uppity." He noticed Ezquiel's pictures plastered above me and wagged a finger. "I knews I was right about you twos. You didn't stays little, did you?"

"Kimaris, I haven't seen Ezequiel since the last time I came across your ugly face. Why are you here?"

"The Old Guy wants to sees you."

Sweat dampened my tee shirt. Kimaris belched, his presence too real. I might not wake up from this nightmare, but I would *not* let him push me around.

I rubbed my arms to comfort myself. "Look here, Mr. Goon, deliver a message from me: Forget it."

Kimaris's laughter vibrated with such ferocity the water in Goldie's bowl splashed against the sides. "Girlie, that ain'ts happening."

I screamed in frustration and threw a boot across the room. Down the hole it went. And up it came back, flying across the room and hitting me in the head.

"Ouch." I rubbed my forehead. "What's the deal with the boots, anyway?"

"Peace offering. The Old Guy remembers how much you likes them. At least he remembers part of the time. His old lady had me search Lily's apartment."

I thanked the On-High that Lily wasn't in the house. "I was nine when I wanted go-go boots, Kimaris."

"Look, the Old Guy wants you to wears them."

"Is he some kind of pervert?" Dumb question. "No way in…" I stopped myself before I used the H word. I hopped off the bed and picked up both boots. I flung one down the hole again, waited a moment, and when it didn't get regurgitated I hurled the other.

I pointed to my closet. "Get out of my room. Now."

Kimaris raised up. Man, that goon was huge. "If you says so." He only needed a step to grab me and put me under his arm. He carried me to the edge of the precipice.

"And aways we go."

He dropped me and down I went. My matchbook, with my last ticket to get back home, lay inside the Herman's Hermits album under my bed banished along with Bobby Sherman.

I landed with my feet inside my go-go boots, with only Minnie Mouse on my tee shirt to protect me.

My bedroom lamp cast a stream of light that didn't quite reach me. Kamiris's voice tumbled down. "And now I waits for that nephew of mine."

The platform where the Burning Sands supplies used to be loaded had toppled over. Broken crates and shards of glass littered the ground. Among the debris, a paper rested underneath the cushion of what might have been a barstool. I bent down and pulled it out.

The faint light coming down the hall that led to Room 777 revealed Bo's beautiful cursive across the page.

Welcome...

The rest of the page had been torn off.

It's your fault, Charlotte.

Mom's voice?

My jackal sauntered down the hall and sat at the edge of the broken glass. *Imagine how much better the world would have been if you'd never been born.*

The paper dropped from my fingers. "Leave me alone."

Oh, I will. In time. But you must follow me first.

The eyes in the wall were gone, only sockets left from where they'd been extracted. A withered ear hung here and there, dead and gray. We turned in a different direction from Ezequiel's old digs in the mailroom, not a demon in sight until we came across a sour-faced one leaning in a crevice scratching her belly with black fingernails. The jackal hissed. The demon lumbered off the way we'd come.

The jackal led me down a rickety staircase with geysers boiling on either side. I had a flashback to when my family visited the Mormon Tabernacle, and I tried to trash Rhonda's paper. On the same trip, we went to Yellowstone. The pools here were like

Mammoth Hot Springs, only with desperate screams and no handrails to protect me if I lost my step.

Down we went, until we reached a bog. Clumps of rocks around us resembled petrified trolls. My boots grew heavy from the muck. I'd been here before with Rhonda, and after more slogging, we came to the pool Bo had gallantly escorted Rhonda and me across. Yes, there, on the other side, lay the passage to his lair. My jackal skirted the pool. If I could get across, disappear through the cracks in the rocks on the other side and jump in a dresser drawer, perhaps I'd find a way home.

The jackal swung her head back and bared her teeth. *Don't you even think about it. You'd only run into Kimaris again.* She shook her head as though she waited impatiently for me to be taken off her hands. *You're an idiot, Charlotte.*

Yep, I played into Kimaris ugly hands. My heavy boots rubbed against the back of my heels as we left the pool behind us and began to climb up another set of questionable stairs. Scalding water trickled down the rock walls, catching the light of torches mounted into them.

I slipped and landed hard on my hands and knees. Rising gingerly, I banged my boots on the step ahead of me, kicking off muck from the soles. I turned to look behind me. In the distance, the bog's terrain mixed with the yellow steam from the geysers.

How long had we been walking? No way to know. Hell didn't run on Pacific Standard Time.

I followed the wake of the jackal's accusations.

Your sister always looked out for you. When have you protected her?

Remember when you broke the cookie jar lid and blamed it on Bo?

If you'd been a good girl, your parents wouldn't have fought. God would have fixed things.

You are so slow.

So clumsy.

So dumb.

You wished your father would die.

I pressed against the gravity of my wretchedness, too tired to resist her word, dragging my legacy and the entire history of the Jackson family behind me.

My jackal waited at the top. She shook the drool from her mouth. Plenty *of room for you in Hell.*

Across the expanse, bright streams of lava etched the face of a brooding mountain holding in Hell from the other side. To my left, an elevator descended to a line of glass windows perched above the plain.

My boots squeezed my legs harder. "Are we done taking the scenic route?"

My jackal yawned and stretched. *Demons used to be thick as fleas. Even up here, they patrolled. But most are gone to Earth now, and humans are on their own in this realm. They don't realize it.* She showed her teeth. *I tire of you.*

She led me down arid switchbacks, zigzagging under a musky sky, neither day nor night, hues of gray, brown, dirty purple rippling like an oil spill above our heads. I limped along until we reached a wide spot jutting from the path with a sign posted saying *Viewing Area*. A melange of cries and shouts, scraping metal, and a constant simmer of fire rose like a pulse.

A telescope had been mounted on a crumbling wall. I stood on the loose rubble and looked through it. Yes, an elevator ran from the pit up to the glass windows etched with *Purgatory Cafe*. I made out a sign beside it like the one at the DMV when Mom got her driver's license, except the number displayed was in the millions.

230,457,923? Hard to read from so far away.

I turned the scope to the platform where demons had tossed people into the fire falls.

One, two, and aways...

No demons now, but someone—man or woman, I wasn't sure—stood at the edge and toppled over.

I whipped the scope down. Where was Ezequiel? What happened to Daddy?

I noticed a movement of blue then.

The jackal placed its front feet on the wall. *Adjust the scope.*

I turned the gear next to my eye. Police uniforms. Officers patrolled like prison guards, snaking through the mass of civilian souls, extending far beyond my vision.

I panned higher and saw that towers the color of dust spread through the chamber. Hideous creatures with skin like armor and large plated heads manned them. I turned the gear tightly to focus on a dumb brutal face that spoke of instinctive evil. Kimaris would have been on the college track in comparison.

Fiends. The jackal landed on all fours. *Watching the watchers. But even they have no power anymore. They just continue to do what they have always done.*

Daddy had to be in that long line of blue, didn't he?

And I am watching you. Move along.

"I can barely walk."

Your fault.

Why would any of this be my fault? Yet, her words sank into the well of remorse growing from the scar the worm had left, the place from where I'd hurt Rhonda, my mom and myself.

After millennia of descent, we became part of the throng. *Number 763,627,632* rang out in the cacophony.

"Tis I! Forsooth, this heavy wait is complete."

A line of cops marched in front of the elevator door. One stepped out and escorted a woman in the tatters of a dress that suggested she died around the time of the Tudors. Her skin had turned a ghastly shade of gray. The crowd pressed on the line of police, but they stood firm, allowing only the woman to enter the elevator. As soon as the door closed, it shot up to the cafe.

Red and yellow, black and white...

The tune I learned from attending a rare Sunday school class played in my head. Monotheistic Hell, is that what Kimaris called the place? Shades of men dressed like they'd walked right out of *The Ten Commandments,* their bodies almost immaterial, huddled in a circle beneath one of the dusty towers rising on knoll behind the crowd. Closer by, a man in a turban stared at the number clutched in his hand, chanting *176,843,512* like a prayer. A large black man in a purple robe sat on the ground, holding his head in his hands. A little old woman with the sweetest face muttered things that would have made Connie blush. Multiply these souls by a million. Toss in some exponents to the 10th power.

Most of the crowd stood silently, gazing at the number machine. A few wandered off with heads down. My jackal wove between the police and those who waited to see if their number might come up.

Number 398,589,455.

"Bingo!" A cowboy raised his hand. The line of officers braced themselves as a unit as the mass pressed forward again, trying to break through and get a free ride to purgatory.

The captain once again stepped from the line to retrieve the lucky soul.

"Daddy!"

He'd gotten a promotion.

Daddy winced in pain. "Charlotte, you aren't supposed to be here."

He was sober. His head was intact!

Blues of joy, pinks of relief, warm yellow like the sun washed over me, but they mixed with memories of ink black nights of never ending arguments and yellow-green fear that made my muscles clench when he drove drunk as I tried to steer the car with my mind. Inevitably, the colors swirled into mucky brown.

The jackal snarled. *It will be your fault if he decides to go to the fire falls.*

She started running.

"I'll find you again, Daddy, I promise."

Daddy's voice echoed behind me now. "No. Don't come back for me."

I had no control over my legs. The boots pulled me in one painful stride after the other, following the jackal who parted the crowd like Charlton Heston. Hands reached out and stroked me as if I were a token of good luck. I was alive, and they were greedy.

My jackal stopped suddenly. A circle of about twenty police officers guarded a massive door like a monolith hewn from aged and the petrified wood of misery.

My boots froze. I toppled into a police woman with a badge pinned to her chest with Tōkyō engraved upon it. She grunted, set me on my feet again, then stepped away.

Good riddance. I hope never to see your pathetic face again.

The jackal bared her teeth and vanished.

The policewoman took a skeleton key off her belt and unlocked it. She pushed her shoulder into the door. It opened with a moan.

"Satan will be with you shortly."

In the cozy room, air conditioning had been turned on, but a fire also burned inside a hearth on the wall across from me. A large relief map hung above the mantle. To my right, a picture window filled the wall giving a panoramic view of the route I'd taken. The switchbacks the jackal led me down looked like broken pieces of spaghetti. On my left, an armchair sat next to an elegant table with a green lamp. Some documents fanned across its top. Behind this, a dark red drape covered a long window.

Thick walls blocked the hubbub of Hell. I hobbled over to study the map. Hell's perimeter reminded me of Australia's. I climbed on the ledge in front of the hearth and touched a star. A "you are here" sign?

The vast plain I'd crossed took up most of the top half of the map. A label that read *Purgatory was* set into a ridge indicating the cliff where the cafe perched. A much larger fold separated Hell Central from a gray expanse—the bog. Behind that, industrial-like squares were etched into the map where the mailroom and the warren of hallways had to be located.

My house sat somewhere above the complex.

At the bottom of the map, a thicker, higher ridge colored dark purple ran along the edge. Painted red lines glowed down the flanks. The fire falls?

The upper righthand corner was labeled Tartarus. Bumps grew higher, pointier, until they reached Tophet, covered in white paint and ragged as the Himaylayas.

An ocean of blue surrounded Hell. Oceans of air, perhaps? One word floated like a little piece of driftwood far off the coast. I raised myself up as far as my boots would allow me.

Paradise.

Below the mass of the map, a long black rectangle stretched the entire length like a buried vault. It was labeled *Underhell*. I reached out and touched the word.

"I made the Underhell to put the Nazis in. I did a good job with it, didn't I, my love?"

The voice wheezed, more air than spoken words.

"Yes, dear."

I pivoted. A beautiful woman stood behind a wicker wheelchair where a fragile, ancient demon was strapped in a seatbelt. His leathery arms were almost black from bruises, though his face and bald pate had the hue of a Red Delicious apple. Were those horns, or did his scalp have a skin condition?

The woman had an aquiline face etched with wrinkles. Wavy hair white as sugar flowed to her elbows. "Who are you, and what are you doing here?"

"Kimaris told me you wanted me. I'm Charlotte Jackson."

The Old Guy's head popped up. "Connie Jackson?"

"No, I'm Charlotte, her sister, and I don't want to be here."

"Evie?" The Old Guy's voice gave out. He struggled to inhale. "Do you think Abraxas is on to our operation?"

I had enough experience to guess the identity of Evie. She pushed the wheelchair across the room to the table and lowered herself slowly into a chair by the table. She motioned for me to come closer.

I wasn't able to take another step. "These boots don't fit me. My feet are on fire." Probably not the smartest thing to say. "Why do you think I'm my sister?"

Evie opened a drawer and took out a pair of reading glasses in the coolest shade of turquoise. She placed the pile of papers on her lap.

"Yes or no. Are you Connie Jackson?"

"No, I'm Charlotte Jackson."

She studied the one on top. "You are fifteen years old?"

"Not for another month."

She took a pen from behind her left ear, not there a moment before, and scribbled on the page. "You like Camels."

"The animal?"

"The cigarette." She sounded impatient. "And you freaked on some bad acid not too long ago."

"No, I'm Charlotte. Connie is my big sister. My mom never lets me out of her sight, even if I wanted to smoke or do drugs. Why did you bring me here?"

Satan had drifted asleep, but my irritating tone must have woken him. His eyes were rheumy, a word I didn't even know I knew, but one that fit perfectly.

"I used to be a lawyer, did you know that? I helped my Evie in her defense when she and Adam were kicked out of the garden. I lost." He glanced around the room as though there were others listening. "I used to be a Cherub. I guarded heaven. Bet you didn't know that either."

Did that explain the police presence?

Evie reached over and patted his hand. "Satie, darling, let me take care of this. This paper says you took a paper from Hell in the Earth year 1965?"

"You're not going to hold that against me. I was only a fourth grader."

"And, you are currently working as a prostitute on Fremont Street?"

Oh, God, the truth about Connie. "No, not me."

Aching feet or not, I hobbled over and ripped the paper from Evie's hand and saw Connie's name printed on top with my birthday. Our lives had been conflated.

"This is a mess. Ezequiel would never have allowed this. I'd have a word with the girl who took over for him in the file room."

Satan's fingers played on the blanket on his lap. "I was a lawyer in Heaven. Did I tell you that? And I cleaned up Heaven more than once. That's what Cherubs do. And I made the Underhell for the Nazis."

Evie sighed. "A long time ago, honeybunch. The question is what are we going to do with this girl. She isn't safe."

I knew exactly what I wanted. "You can start by helping me get these boots off."

Satan leaned over so far he'd have fallen out of his chair if it hadn't been for the seatbelt. "I thought you liked go-go boots."

"Not since *Get Smart* got canceled."

He chuckled, reached down and took off his house shoe. "Ring, ring."

"Kimaris said you sent them back to me."

Evie tapped her pencil on the table. "No, those boots were Lilith's originally. Abraxas and Kimaris should have never given them to you in the first place."

"Do I know Lilith, Evie?"

Evie reached over and patted Satie's hand. "Adam did. And when you were on the dark side, you did too." She frowned. "You knew her *very* well."

The Old Guy began snoring. Evie put her pencil on the table and crossed her legs. "Charlotte, Abraxas took Ezequiel up to Burning Sands, but Ezequiel did work for us for a while. You're right. He would have never gotten you and your sister mixed up.

He made an arrangement with us that if anyone in your family needed help, he'd order the paperwork from the filing room to see what we might be able to do. We have some connections."

"You didn't send Kimaris to get me?"

"We didn't."

My feet must have been horribly swollen. The boots pinched even tighter. I moaned.

Evie reached over and nudged Satan awake again. "Can you help her? The boots are the wrong size. Abraxas is up to his old tricks."

"What?"

She spoke louder. "Can you help her get these torture devices off her feet?" She gestured to me. "Here, take my chair." She walked behind Satan's wheelchair as I took her seat. She pushed him closer to me. "Give him your leg. Right one first."

What did I have to lose? He reached over and mumbled in a language that sounded like Martian. He took the boot off and set it down next to his wheelchair. I gave him my left.

"It's been so long since I've done something kind with my own hands."

Evie walked to the drape and held the cord. "We've been trying to help people get out of Hell for the last two thousand years. Since Ezequiel brought your father here, we're finding more and more souls who never should have come in the first place. We're even bypassing purgatory for a few of them. If we can, we get them into Heaven."

The old man whined. "I want to go back to Heaven."

"I know, Satie."

She pulled back the drapes revealing an emerald green golf course. Several oak trees blazed in full fall radiance. I'd only seen the like in books or on TV, never in Vegas. A small man with coffee colored skin swung at a ball on a tee. He missed, but his shoulders shook with laughter.

A woman walked over a knoll in smart white pants and a crisp yellow shirt. She looked like Lily.

"Mary?"

"And her son."

"Jesus golfs?"

"We enjoy watching him. He's also a heck of a surfer."

Satan stared at Jesus and with a great deal of effort raised his hand and waved. Jesus rocked back and forth on his feet, readying for another swing. He didn't see us watching but Mary did. She gave a thumbs up.

Evie offered one back to her. "I just love her. By the way, did you know I finally dumped Adam after the whole Cain and Abel disaster?"

I didn't.

"Satie is my soulmate. After the horrible things we caused—" She paused. "Well, after the stories were spread about us, Jesus treated us kindly, even with that wretched crucifixion. Somehow, he carved out this apartment in the middle of Hell for us."

I kissed her cheek. "I don't know my grandma in Indiana very well. I'd like to think you could be a grandma."

"Thank you, dear Charlotte."

I knelt and took Satan's withered hand.

He startled for a moment, but then smiled. He must have had dentures because his teeth looked as good as Bo's. "I'm so glad things got mixed up so we had the opportunity to meet you, Connie."

Evie and I spoke in tandem. "Charlotte."

I let go of his hand. "How do you send people to Heaven?"

Satan turned lucid. "We ask your father to find the ones we feel took a wrong turn. Before he came there were other captains. They got their reward eventually. We pretend we're going to do awful things to cover our tracks. They're terrified when they step into the apartment, but boy do they smile when they figure out what's up."

"Daddy's working undercover?"

"It's what he does well."

I didn't feel so charitable. "I hope he knows what hell he created in my family."

"He does. He won't forget." Satan made a frowny face. "I can't forget what I've done."

I placed my palm on the glass. "After you bring people here, how do you get them on the other side of the window?"

Evie offered me the chair again, but I didn't want to sit. "We tap on it. Jesus shows up. In the meantime, we have a nice cup of tea, maybe some scones. They won't believe they're forgiven. But they take his word for it."

"And then what?"

"The window opens, and they hop through it. Would you like a cup of tea?"

I shook my head. "You haven't tapped for Jesus for yourselves?"

Evie placed her hand close to mine. "Satie has an issue with pride. He says he wants to go. But when I say, 'Let's do it,' he gets incredibly agitated."

Mary shifted back and forth at the tee with her club, and Jesus talked into something like a Star Trek Communicator.

I tapped on the window. He didn't hear me, so I banged on it.

He put the communicator in his shirt pocket and walked over. The window dissolved and a sweet summer breeze hit my face.

"You're not due for a long time."

I cut to the chase. "Can't these two have a pass? Throw them back through the window if they don't behave."

Jesus stared into my eyes. All I wanted to do was look back at him. His smile seemed a little sad, but a wave of relief passed from him to me. "Connie, I've been waiting a long time for someone to ask. Hey, Satie, want to finish the round with me?"

Even Jesus couldn't keep my sister and me straight, but I forgave him. He stepped through the window like he'd done it a thousand times. He picked up the Old Guy who screamed, "No!" from the wheelchair and carried him to Heaven.

Jesus set him down by Mary's feet. She made her swing and bonked his head.

"Ouch!"

Mary bonked him again. "Serves you right for treating my son so badly."

Satie's wings unfolded. He looked at peace, and 6,000 years younger.

Evie turned to me. "I never considered forcing the issue. I hate to leave you alone, but there will be help and all will be well eventually."

She stepped through and her body changed to what it must have been like in the Garden. Let's say vavavoom! Jesus's cheeks turned red.

Who knew Paradise and Perdition were separated by a pane of glass? I flopped in the chair. I needed to find Daddy, but exhaustion pressed down on me.

The edges of what looked like Poloroids poked out beneath the pile of papers. I slid them out. Connie, dressed in pink hot pants and white boots with spiked heels, wasn't alone. Hayden

Nelson, now husband to Millie, held her shoulders and bent his head close to hers.

That bastard!

I hoped the Old Guy and Evie were having a grand old time. Maybe they'd have drinks with Jesus and his mom and hatch up plans to make a better Earth. In the meantime, Abraxas wanted my sister. He controlled Vegas, aimed at being in charge of the whole state of Nevada, and I bet he had intentions on the White House.

For me? Kimaris knew my location and Hayden was up to no good with Connie. I glanced at the go-go boots. The left one began tapping the floor, impatient for the rest of my story to unfold.

The Beast

The golf party disappeared over the knoll. A soft shower settled itself on the grass, coloring it an iridescent teal. The limbs of the autumnal trees danced. A rain of amber, gold, and scarlet leaves blew across the lawn, carpeting it like jewels. The windowpane seemed as thin as the width of a hair. I leaned against it the way I did when, as a very little girl, I tried to step through the full-length mirror on my parent's bedroom closet to reach the other Charlotte who mimicked me.

I wanted to throw the lamp against the window to break it and go home through a path in Heaven, but I'd grown up enough to know the act would be useless. My way home would be difficult and dangerous. I needed to find Daddy again, and I had to rescue Connie from the fingers of Hayden and the other men who used her. I had no idea how, but I had to try.

The boots grew impatient with my reluctance to leave the sanctuary of Satan's apartment. They marched themselves to the door and stomped like a two-year-old having a tantrum.

"Okay, already. I'm coming."

The boots stood at attention. I had to trust that they'd lead me to where I next needed to go. I left the picture on the table, walked across the room and turned the doorknob.

The residue of my jackal's energy engulfed me. Inside the industrial drone of Hell, I felt dirty and hopeless once again.

3,765,329,438

The ecstatic voice of a boy shouted, "That's my number!"

A kid dressed in overalls waved his ticket in the air. He didn't seem older than ten. How long had he endured here?

Earlier, when the numbers had been announced, I'd been too overwhelmed with the chaos to be aware of the bleak moans of those who were left. I felt caught in quicksand, but then one of the boots kicked me in the butt.

I tried to find the woman who'd escorted me, but a new shift of the Deceased Police had come on duty. A few possibilities passed through my mind of why these officers had been sent here and not to Heaven, or at least purgatory. Did they beat suspects until they confessed? Did they cheat on their taxes? Covet their neighbor's vacations to Hawaii? Not honor their mothers and fathers?

I had to stop speculating and do something.

The boots walked next to me like a well trained dog. A portly guard, a Keystone Cop kind of officer, who must have been put on Hell duty before my grandmother's time, turned around.

"I need to see Captain Jackson." I ignored the voice my jackal planted in my mind telling me to stop being presumptuous. "I'm on a mission"—dare I claim this?— "from Abraxas."

Officer O'Malley from Scranton, Ohio, if his badge told the truth, tapped his baton into his left palm.

I crossed my fingers. I gave O'Malley a half truth. Abraxas did want me in Hell, didn't he? I had the boots to prove it. "He plans to rain terror on Las Vegas as soon as possible. He's considering putting the captain back on the payroll at the Burning Sands. You can talk to me or to Kimaris, your choice."

A slight bit of pride lifted me from complete self-loathing. If nothing else, I hadn't lost my imagination. But then I slammed down into my well of doubt again. Office O'Malley would see through me. How could a barefooted fourteen year-old girl in a tee shirt with Minnie Mouse blowing heart kisses intimidate him?

He eyed me skeptically. "Never seen a demon like you before."

I stood tall. "I am an underling in training. Abraxas says he has big plans for me."

If I'd known how prophetic my words were, I'd never have uttered them.

Something possessed me to snap my fingers. "Boots, you're made for walking. Do your job."

They attacked poor Office O'Malley, and, boy, did they get air. He raised his arms to protect his face. "All right, all right. Jackson is off duty. I'll take you to his cell."

It seemed Daddy spent his off duty time at the Big House. O'Malley led me to an ugly concrete block of a building carved into the cliff the Purgatory Cafe rested upon. I followed him down a dismal gray hallway lit with fluorescent lights, the boots clomping behind me. We passed iron cages, cells like the ones I'd seen in a dozen movies. Police officers sat on bunks covered by navy blue blankets watching televisions, but none of them had any rabbit ears. How did they get reception? The TVs rested on metal tables like ones I'd seen on detective shows where people's bodies lay with tags on their toes.

We finally came to Daddy's place. O'Malley pushed the bars on his door, and it swung open. No key needed.

O'Malley stood outside, his feet wide apart, staring away from us.

Daddy's coat hung on a hanger that itself hung from a horizontal iron bar near the door. He sat on the edge of a bed with a thin mattress. An ironing board lined up along the wall to my right. Daddy pressed his own clothes now? Mom would never believe it.

He stared at his TV. To one side of it, a rectangular machine hummed. Three overgrown cassettes were stacked on the other side with a legal sized notepad with yellow paper and a PaperMate in front of them. Daddy pushed a button and a fourth cassette popped through a slot in the machine. He took it out and immediately put in the cassette on top of the pile. The machine swallowed it.

"Daddy?" He'd put out a finger to push the button but his hand froze. I slipped between the coroner's table and the bed to be next to him. "A lot has happened back home since you've been gone."

He wouldn't look at me. "Charlotte, why are you here?"

I didn't know where to begin. With a game of Concentration six years ago? Helping Ezequiel and having fun riding the ladders in the mailroom? The worm and the jackal wearing me down? Or Kimaris throwing me over the ledge of my closet?

He didn't seem anxious for a reply. He peered at the TV. "What is this?"

"It's called a VCR." He pointed to the screen, his large hand, the bony knuckles, the leathery skin,, the ridges on the nail of his index finger were all so familiar. "Like a movie projector, except it uses a type of cassette tape instead of film."

He leaned his head closer. A woman with chestnut hair in a dress that hung like a sack held a baby in a rocking chair. She seemed as thin as Rhonda.

"That's my mother. I don't remember her." The scene shifted to his father holding a belt and striking him. My body jerked with each wallop. I reached over and took Daddy's hand that rested on his knee. I watched him as a teenager, no older than me, raise a glass of amber liquid to his lips. His eyes closed and his face relaxed.

"I could never stop, Charlotte."

Daddy pushed the FF button and the tape sped up. He stopped it when Mom held a screaming baby, Connie, I think, not me, her pose almost like his mother's. Mom looked so tired. And then one scene after another followed: bruises, yelling, silent periods of pins and needles, tension reaching to the moon and back. These contrasted with sober episodes at the police department in situations I never knew about: guns held on him, beatings he received, putting handcuffs on men whose faces had no souls, and women who might have been twenty-five, but looked fifty. All hollowed eyed. Daddy's were too, until he reached for the Jim Beam. For a second, the same look of peace passed over his face as it had with his first drink.

Ezequiel had to watch the car accident when his sister died over and over. He felt helpless to look away. Would I be shown videos of all the times I hurt people when I became damned? The fire option might be kinder.

"Daddy, stop, you don't have to keep watching." But I fell into a trance as Daddy's life played out in front of me. Why were only the bad times saved? What about when he took me and Connie to Ringling Brothers and bought us cotton candy? Or when we played Chinese Checkers on Saturday mornings when the house was at peace?

But no. I watched myself sipping a strawberry milkshake. Daddy began to sob. "I'm sorry, Charlotte."

I remembered the shake gave me no joy, and how Connie held me on my bed as my parents' fight seemed like it would never end.

The scene on the TV froze, and a soft beep, beep, beep came from the VCR.

Ezequiel appeared in living color, dressed in the finely tailored business suit, wearing a ruby tie, his hair wavy and black, falling to his shoulders. He stared at one of the Star Trek thingies Jesus had used and didn't look up.

The boots that had stayed at attention next to Officer O'Malley scampered back down the hall.

I wanted to cry out "Ezequiel" so much I almost choked on his name. I clenched the cold steel of the table with both hands. I refused to act like a teenage girl with a crush. Besides, O'Malley still stood outside the cell.

Ezequiel's voice was almost a whisper. "*347,905,312. Rafael Guzman Valdez.*"

Daddy wrote down the number and the name as Ezequiel filled in the details.

"Guzman cheated on his wife a couple of times, and then regretted it to the end of his days. He worked as a city planner and made major improvements in sanitation in the slums of Madrid. He died fighting Franco's army in 1936. I negotiated the pardon. Be ready for about 100 Burning Sands clients to arrive. Escort them to the fire falls, give them a good scare, and then let them figure out where they belong. Usual routine, Walt."

Were the new recruits being marched through my bedroom that very moment now the hole had breached open again? There had to be alternative routes, didn't there?

I held my breath. Hoping Ezequiel would look up.

He did. His lips formed an O in surprise. His head turned from side to side as though to make sure no one watched.

"I've missed you so much, Ezequiel." So much for playing it cool. "Kimaris pushed me down here. I met Satan and Eve. They're with Jesus now. How can I get back to Las Vegas and help Connie?"

Daddy switched off the TV.

"What's happened to Connie?"

Daddy's vision must have improved because the big thick glasses he wore on Earth were gone. For the few minutes I'd been with him, I'd managed to hide the place in my heart the worm had chewed. I let in false hope and the pretty once-upon-a-time stories where all would be well. I trusted the promise Mary gave me, and I trusted the tiny seed of hope Eve left before she climbed into Heaven.

I understood now how things were. The dead core in my soul broke these fantasies. I rose up fast, hitting my thighs hard on the edge of the table. I didn't yelp but used the pain to fuel me.

"You're asking what happened to her, Daddy? Now? You never cared when you were alive. You didn't care about anything except your whiskey and that deformed brother of mine. You were so caught up with the stupid delusion Mommy was fooling around, you were blind to how much trouble Connie was falling into, even when you got her out of it. And now, every sin you were convinced Mommy had committed, Connie is doing them, only worse."

Daddy put his head in his hands and sobbed.

So pathetic.

The jackal hadn't disappeared. She had hid deeper inside me. She opened the place where my last demon began to form, only an embryo but growing fast. I named her The Beast as I stood in front of Daddy and watched him cry.

The scuffling soles of the go-go boots beat down the hall. A few seconds behind them, the squish-squish of Kimaris's steps approached.

Kimaris slurped into view on the other side of the bars. He jerked his thumb. "Scram."

Officer O'Malley followed orders. Kimaris walked into the cell. He gave one look at Daddy and gave a rolling laugh. In his right hand he clutched the mini dress Connie had worn to the Elvis concert. He threw it at me. I let it fall to the floor.

"Puts its on nows."

My beast grew in my belly. "You're sick, Kimaris. Going through a girl's private things."

"Your sister at least has a more interesting inventory than you ever dids. Don't you want to live a bit? You put the dress on now."

Daddy continued to cry into his hands. Kimaris eyed me, waiting for me to take off my clothes.

"Turn around, you goon."

He snickered but did so. "Yeah, I gaves a talk to Bo. Straightened him right out, I tells you."

I faced the wall with the ironing board, slipped off my top, and put the dress over my head. Thank goodness Connie was taller than me because the dress fell to the top of my knees, giving me some modesty. I slipped out of my cut-offs.

"Okay."

Kimaris turned back and snapped his fingers. The boots hurried over.

"Now these. Back on. They fits now."

"No way. I couldn't walk in them."

He snapped the fingers of his other hand. "There, now they fit."

"Okay, okay." I shoved my legs into them. "Make them looser, Kimaris. Jesus Christ."

Kimaris grabbed his head and screamed. The prison rocked like an earthquake hit it. Light and fresh air flooded through the cell for the briefest of moments. Daddy looked up, his face clear now. He hid the piece of paper with the number on it under the VCR.

Kimaris's eyes narrowed into slits, and he let out a fart with doom and gloom written all over it. "Don't you ever say that again, girlie."

He clenched my arm. I was so over him roughing me up. My beast kicked me in the belly. My mind became cold. I'd do what I had to do. I'd survive this, and I'd pay him back someday.

"Make these boots another size bigger, and I'll follow you anywhere. Don't you call me girlie ever again."

"It's a deal." He smiled. "Cupcake."

Words that Mom would hate to hear me say flew out of my mouth. Daddy reared up and shoved Kimaris out of the way. Kimaris growled but stepped back.

Daddy took my shoulders and kissed my forehead. Leaning down, he looked at me with a cold sober expression.

"Get out of here and never come back. You do not deserve to be here. Now, or ever. Too many people have condemned themselves. You don't have to, Charlotte. Do you know what I'm talking about?"

I told him I did as my beast grew. I knew whose voice I'd obey.

Daddy took a step back. "You've grown up. You look—"

"Like a whore? Like a goddamn tramp? Like the awful things you called Mom?"

He shook his head. "No, no, you're my beautiful daughter. Please forgive me for everything I've done."

I got Satan out of Hell, but then I held nothing personal against him. No forgiveness lay inside of me. I refused to be vulnerable and give Daddy what he needed. I teetered at the edge, but my beast clawed at my back. Each cell of my body understood the conclusion Bo had come to. Love hurts too much.

I said nothing, one way or the other.

Kimaris watched our interaction play out, smart enough to know to let things take their course. "I gots to takes you back to Vegas. Are you dones with the smoozy parts?"

I nodded. I wouldn't feel guilty. I would leave Daddy. I'd do it now.

"Let's go."

My boots felt fine. I followed Kimaris out of the cell and didn't look back.

"We're going to takes a shortcut."

Another ride, sans elevator or stairs or windy path through geysers, mud holes and corridors. Up we went, sucked through the Earth just like my first return trip when I was nine. Someday, I'd need a lot of therapy.

We emerged through a storm drain in an alley next to the Horseshoe Casino. Horns honked on Fremont Street. Stale tobacco floated up from cast off cigarettes. The outer edge of the alley blinked red, blue, fluorescent green cast by the neon lights that would assault us when we stepped to the street.

We weren't alone, though. In a dark recess, a couple did things Daddy had been paid by the LVPD to stop.

Kimaris slurpy-stepped toward them. "Beat it."

Both of them screamed. They ran to the street without straightening their clothes.

"I havent's lost the old touch." Kimaris pulled me to the street. "Okay, Cupcake, you ares on your own for a while." A black limo pulled up. The door opened by itself. "Sees you around."

He barely fit through the door, but fit he did. The Golden Nugget's lights blazed across the street. Three boys walked with their parents heading towards the Pioneer Club and Vegas Vic like Connie and I used to with Mom and Dad. The boys were pointing to the lights and saying, "Wow," over and over. I followed them.

Before we passed The Mint, a man, a patsy like Daddy pretended to be, blocked my way. The safe passage of traveling behind the family had been an illusion.

"You're sure cute in those boots. How much?" I tried to make my way around him, but he wouldn't let me. "I'm not good enough for you?"

My beast came to my rescue. Heat burned my face, and I felt its muscles twist and transform. The man's face paled. He shoved money into my hand and ran into the casino. I had taxi fare home.

I stumbled to a trashcan and leaned against it. I reached down to take off the boots, but they were glued to my legs. My breath came in gulps, but after a minute, my heart slowed and my face relaxed. My reflection shimmered in a plate glass window in front of me. I looked like a smaller version of Connie, still human, damn it.

Vegas Vic's voice came from above. "Howdy, pardner."

I traced his cowboy outfit past his boots to the street. A woman with long black hair dressed in Levis and a black tee shirt ushered a younger woman into a sedan.

So, this is where Lily ran off each night, turned back into her demon self. She was pimping girls. No more kitty treats for her.

The car took off in my direction. The driver side window rolled down. Captain Hartman was at the wheel.

Hayden? Lily? Hartman? All of them pretending they were good, each one of them living a double life. They would burn in Hell if I had any power at all. I raised my arm to hail a cab. I wanted to go home before the beast took over completely.

"Charlotte, why are you here?"

Jason jaywalked across the street. Cars honked.

A cabby slowed down and yelled, "You crazy or something?"

Jason marched right to me.

I came up with a quick explanation. "I wanted to look for Connie too. But no luck. I want to go home now."

Jason looked up at Vegas Vic as though he expected to receive some advice on how to deal with me, though he might have really been counting to ten. He focused on me again. "There's a ring hunting for young women. Girls, that is. It's not safe for you to be here." He pointed in the direction he wanted me to go. "Mom is taking June to get something to eat. Any luck, I'll get you home before they get back."

In the car, he turned on the radio. The DJ reported thunderstorms were expected. Nothing unusual for early September, and then Carol King started singing about the sky tumbling down.

A streak of lightning zig zagged in front of us.

Jason tapped the steering wheel in time with the music. "Looks like the storm's coming in early."

Thunder boomed so loud I jumped in my seat. "That was close."

Rain pelted the car. Jason turned on the windshield wipers full blast because within seconds the road had disappeared.

"I came home early and got Rhonda and took her to your house. Bo didn't know where you were. He was a mess, like he'd seen a ghost or something. I didn't know what to do, so I went to look for Connie again."

Puddles had grown into lakes along the side of the road. I thought of Ezequiel's accident. "Slow down, will you?"

Jason eased off the pedal. "Rhonda's not doing well."

Rhonda now went to doctors for the opposite reason she used to. My anxiety notched up to a new level. I started to pick at a fingernail. Time to shift the conversation to the place it needed to go.

"Do you trust Hayden?"

Jason turned on his blinker. We pulled onto Sahara Boulevard and passed the Ford Dealership where our moms worked.

"Why?"

I thought about the picture I left on Satan and Eve's table. "He makes me feel uncomfortable."

"He's a good guy, Charlotte. You know, Mom is even thinking of converting. She's pretty pissed off she can't take communion anymore."

I brooded the rest of the way home. Who would believe me if I said Hayden knew where Connie was hiding? Luck wasn't with me in any event. When we got there, both Millie's and Mom's cars were parked in the driveway.

Mom rushed up to me the moment I came through the door. I prepared for the inevitable question.

"Where were you?"

"I wanted to look for Connie too."

Mom stepped back. "What were you thinking?" She scanned me. "And why are you wearing her dress?"

I didn't have time for a long story, so I told her an easier one. "I put on Connie's dress because I wanted to feel close to her."

I walked into the kitchen and opened the refrigerator. Seeing three bottles of Coke made me almost hyperventilate. Mom stood so close behind me when I stepped back, I almost knocked her over.

"Where did you get those boots?"

They weren't invisible anymore.

"In Connie's closet. Look, I'm home. Nothing happened to me. I promise not to do this again."

Mom covered her face. "I can't take this."

I wouldn't feel sorry for her anymore.

Millie called from the living room. "June, come sit down. You need to rest."

Mom reached for my hand. I stood stiffly and kept my arm at my side, but I let her take it. I allowed her "I love you" to pass through me. She shuffled back to Millie in her house shoes.

I wanted to fall asleep, but on my way to bed I tried to find out if Millie knew anything. "Has Hayden called?"

She looked at her watch. "Not yet, but knowing him, he'll look all night for Connie."

Yeah, right.

Bo and Rhonda were whispering in his room, his door halfway closed.

"You have to eat more. Promise me you will."

Rhonda spoke so softly, I didn't hear her answer. I leaned forward a bit to look around. Their arms were wrapped around each other, and their lips pressed together in the way I'd long to press mine against Ezequiel.

I stepped across to my room. Whatever Kimaris did to rough Bo up, he seemed no worse for it. The rain kept pouring. I fell on top of my bed in Connie's dress. My boots were a part of me. I don't know how long I slept when I felt Bo shake me.

"Hey, Charlotte, wake up."

I moaned. "Go away."

"I can take you to Ezequiel."

I jolted from my pillow. "What are you talking about?"

"Kimaris took me to the Burning Sands. He threatened me, but I didn't budge. I didn't let him scare me. He wanted me to go back to work for Daddy Abraxas, but I told him no way. Anyway, I know where Ezequiel is. I think I can get you in and out of the casino without anyone noticing."

My beast paced inside my head. And then it curled up and went to sleep.

Bo held up Mom's keys. "I can get you there."

I pulled my legs to my chest. "You're not old enough to drive."

"Really, Charlotte?"

Okay, technically he had thousands of years on me.

Ezequiel.

I wanted to see him. More than anything I had ever wanted in my life.

"Okay, let's go."

Bo's face lost its smile.

"What's wrong?"

"Kimaris threatened me with the odds for the future. There's a 97 percent chance Rhonda will Karen Carpenter in a few years. He told me he'd reverse them if I worked for him again, but that's bullshit. He's not that powerful."

As awful as Bo used to be, I never heard him swear. I was totally confused.

"She and Jason are going to make hit records?"

Bo shook his head. "Never mind."

Three Demons

"**M**ove your legs."

Bo stuck them straight out. "What are you doing?"

I wiggled as far as I could under the bed and stretched until I found my Herman's Hermit album. I pulled it out, knelt next Bo, and tapped the edge of the cover. The matchbook fell on my sheets.

"I figure if a match can get me out of Hell, it might be good insurance for Burning Sands if something goes wrong."

Bo opened it. "Only one match left."

"If it works…The rest sputtered out the night Kimaris took Ezequiel and me to purgatory."

Bo handed it to me. "The night he got his promotion?"

I nodded.

The wind howled like a wolf as it wrapped around the house. An umbrella would be useless. I got up and stood on tiptoes to reach the top of my closet and a poncho I'd never used.

"Maybe the match will bring you luck. I'll meet you in the garage in five."

I tucked the matchbook between my right calf and the faux leather at the top of the boot. Quick trip to the bathroom. As I washed my hands, my reflection alarmed me. The half moons under my eyes were black. A pimple on my cheek had formed overnight. I felt hopeless.

When I got into the garage, Bo had already backed the car to the driveway. The storm masked the noise. Rain fell in a solid sheet, clear and almost impermeable as Saran Wrap. I lowered the garage door and ran to the car.

As we snaked through our neighborhood, water flowed down gutters and pooled into the streets. Upside down waterfalls fanned to the windows. When Bo pulled on the freeway, rain pelted the windshield harder as our speed increased. The wipers switched back and forth like a metronome. I gripped the armrest, my left fist balled in my lap.

Bo focused on the sleek pavement. Traffic slowed, and the blur of taillights expanded into red coronas. Lightning cut open the sky, and the high rises to the northwest appeared like battlements.

Finally, Bo turned on his signal, and we exited onto Las Vegas Boulevard. At Burning Sands, he parked next to a large bus. On its side, five foot high letters spelled out *Sunny Senior Tours*.

We sat for several moments as the rain pelted the car roof. Bo blew a breath through his lips. "You've been to Hell and back, Charlotte. I don't mean to be funny. I'm sorry about what Uncle Kimaris did to you."

I ran my hands up and down my boots, grateful at least my feet would stay dry when we left the car. "I found Daddy."

"And?"

I told him about my journey and how Daddy tried to do the right considering his circumstances. I didn't tell Bo how I left him.

"Why am I here, Bo? Will Ezequiel even want to see me?

My beast purred in her sleep.

"I'll take you home, if you want."

Bo was so sincere, I wanted to hug him. Going back would be the logical thing to do. We were about to step into Abraxas's palace on Earth.

Las Vegas now.

Carson City in his crosshairs.

Washington.

The world.

I let the rain lull me for a moment. Maybe Ezequiel's voice would comfort me again. I almost felt like the Charlotte I used to be, the little girl who prayed for a guardian angel. Yet, I wanted to feel his lips press against mine. He was now barely a year older than me, minus his time in eternity. If we met in high school, he'd be my boyfriend. I'd wear his leather jacket.

"Charlotte?"

"Let's go, Bo."

We wove between the cars and buses. He steered me to the left of the entrance into a recess in the facade. We pressed our backs against the wall, both of us needing to catch our breath.

Bo took my hand. "I'd do anything for Rhonda, Charlotte. I understand why you came."

We walked deeper into the niche. He reached into the pocket of his peacoat and pulled out a skeleton key.

"How did you get that?"

"From the time I used to hang out here with Daddy Abraxas. He forgot he gave it to me, so I figured why return it? Let's leave our wet clothes here."

I dropped my poncho next to where Bo threw his coat. The key clicked in the lock. The door opened. He put the key into his shirt pocket and reached down to his coat and retrieved a flashlight.

I giggled. "You should have been a Boy Scout."

He gave me a gentle, "Shh."

The door closed slowly behind us, the hinges as silent as my sleeping beast. The beam from his flashlight emitted soft yellow light. We stepped downstairs, then had another descent to negotiate. Someday, I'd figure out a way to get to the top of the tallest building in the world and stay among the clouds all day long.

At the bottom of the stairs, three hallways spread like a fan from a dull space painted industrial gray.

Bo led me down the middle hall. "Demons love their warrens, don't they, Charlotte?"

We passed no doors. The emptiness unnerved me more than the full cavalcade I'd traveled through the previous evening. Our footsteps echoed, and I felt exposed.

"Someone must be watching us."

"Only service goons come this way. Their shifts don't start for a couple of hours."

We finally came to our first door with the word *Accounting* etched into a gold plate.

"What's the thing with your handwriting on everything?"

"I spent a lot of alone time in my place in the bog. I'm an introvert, you know. Daddy Abraxas would send me things to label, messages to write. Kept me busy, and it allowed me to my art." He pointed to the right. "We're going the next door. I told Ezequiel I needed to talk to him, and he suggested this room."

Bo pushed me into a windowless space filled with office supplies.

"Don't touch anything. Some of the pens are pens, but sometimes they turn into things you don't want to know about. Don't get me started on the Scotch tape. I'll be back in a minute."

I stood in the middle of the room hugging myself. What had I done? In my last moments, I'd be impaled on a paper cutter? I put my hands to my face. Ezequiel was going to see me with bad hair and a pimple.

My tears fell. Bad hair, a pimple, and puffy red eyes.

I didn't feel the door open or close, but I sensed Ezequiel behind me. I braced for him to say, "What are you doing here?" but that's not what happened.

He gently turned me in a half circle until I faced him. He studied my face. I wanted to turn away, but his brown eyes held me.

"You're fifteen?"

I didn't mince for three weeks. I nodded.

Ezequiel stood there more beautiful than I remembered, though stubble now covered his chin. His hair had grown even longer than when I'd seen him in the casino, flowing in waves down his back. He dressed in the same smart business suit, tie, ruby clasp and cufflinks he wore the night Daddy died.

He studied my face like he didn't know me anymore.

My heart nearly broke. "I'm the same Charlotte."

He smiled slightly like he knew that was no longer true. How many times had I kissed him in my imagination? And now he was this close, it felt utterly impossible. Even if I'd kissed another boy before, it would be impossible.

But there in Hell on Earth, a miracle happened.

"I've missed you so much, Charlotte."

Ezequiel circled me with his arms and held me. He loved me too. Real love was so simple, beyond romance, or duty, or brotherly affection.

His breath tickled my face. "When Bo said you were here, I didn't believe it. That brother of yours is clever to get through our defenses. But you have to go. You're too good to be here."

I put my hand on his chest and pushed back. "No, I'm not good. You don't know what I've done."

"Release Satan and Eve? Giving your father some hope? Pissing off Abraxas big time? I have been this close to you, Charlotte, all of the time."

He touched my forehead with his lips.

A point of light, like the one I'd seen from Bo's secret room, danced like a torch on the wall. The cruel room vanished. We stood in a garden, an apple tree blossoming with baby-white petals, poplar trees reaching toward the sky behind us, and beyond them, rolling hills covered by emerald grass. In the distance, a river cascaded over boulders and a songbird sang a wistful melody.

Ezequiel's wings unfolded, the light in them seemed to be filtered through sunflower petals. They were far more splendid than anything I had imagined.

A voice, impossible to tell whether a man's or woman's, became part of the light, each word grounding me with peace. "This is what is real, Charlotte. Only love."

"It's so beautiful."

"What is?"

The garden disappeared with his question, and we were again standing in a cramped supply room full of peril. Ezequiel brushed his lips against mine but pulled back immediately.

No, Ezequiel, don't stop. "What's wrong?"

"This is impossible. Next year you'll be sixteen."

"I'll have caught up with you."

"But, Charlotte, you're going to keep getting older, and I'm going to stay sixteen for at least another five hundred years."

I didn't want logic. I wanted this moment to last forever.

He tried to step back, but I wouldn't let him. "Go home, and don't come back. Forget about me."

Not that easy, Ezequiel. You don't know how stubborn I've become.

"If I didn't forget about you before, why would I now? Besides, Connie's missing, and Lily's up to something. I need you as much as ever.'"

Ezequiel lifted my chin. We kissed again. I started to tingle. I wanted to show him that I knew a thing or two, but he wouldn't let me put my tongue in his mouth.

He pulled back. "No, no."

His wings were gone. "Where are they?"

"What?"

"Your wings. Rhonda saw them at Daddy's funeral and a few moments ago I did when we were in Heaven."

The door swung open. Bo's gaze lingered on Ezequiel. He'd changed so much I never knew what to expect with him, but clearly something was wrong.

Ezequiel put his hand on my back. I fixed its warmth and pressure in my memory.

"Get Charlotte back home safely."

Bo's face crumpled in tears. "I can't. Don't you know by now you can never trust a demon?"

Abraxas pushed him to the side, elegantly dressed as ever. His cape flowed around him like a black sea, his hair white as the Arctic in winter.

Ezequiel didn't look away from the demon-lord. "Charlotte, did you bring the matches?"

I reached into the top of my boot. "I only have one."

"Light it. Fast."

I whispered a quick prayer that the match would work and striking it would bring both Ezequiel and me home. My hands trembled as I brushed it across the rumpled strip. Somehow it managed to spark.

Sulfur stung my nostrils. I landed on my hands and knees on top of my bed. Ezequiel hadn't come with me.

Never trust a demon.

Bo was such an actor, faking concern for Rhonda, pretending he cared about what happened to Ezequiel and me. He'd cast a spell on Rhonda. Evil through and through, encouraged her to starve. I didn't care how much he cried.

Whom might I trust? Not Mom, Connie, Heyden, Lily. Not Captain Hartman who always seemed so nice. Not even Rhonda. I wished my parents had settled in San Bernardino or Phoenix. Better yet, why not Nome where the legions of Hell might think twice about visiting?

Kimaris peaked above the hole in my closet. Rage creased his face. He crawled over the rim, and his hands grabbed me before I got out of his way. He picked me up, slammed me against the wall covered by my drawings of Ezequiel and held me there with my feet dangling.

"You ain'ts so clever, Cupcake. Don't thinks a little matchie will save you for what Abraxas gots planned. I'ms paying you this little visit to lets you know that boyfriend and daddy of yours have beens found out. No mores saintly operations. They gets to decide between the fire falls or the underhell."

Dental floss. He needed dental floss badly, but I wouldn't be deterred.

"You don't have the key to the underhell. It's in Heaven with Jesus."

His face mottled into the shade of a three day old bruise. Mentioning Jesus poked a sore spot. "Don'ts you forget. I knows where your sister is, and I knows who your friends are. Remembers that. And believes you me, Ezequiel and Bo ain'ts in Paradise."

I made a fist and brought it up to his face. "Where's Connie?"

He snickered and let go.

I fell on my bed. "Your feet stink."

Pow! I'd landed another blow. Kimaris's bruised face scrunched like I'd scorched him with an iron. "That's what Lily told me. You females—"

Who would have known he was so sensitive about his feet?

"You little bitch in your sister's dress. Do you knows what she's done wearing that thing?" He gave me graphic details. "You're no different in those fuck-me boots you wanted so badly. If Bo hadn't come back to the supply closet when he dids, you'd be on your hands and knees with Ezequiel, just like now."

He flipped me over and pushed up my dress.

My beast woke and I roared. I mule kicked him where it hurt. Who knew goons were as sensitive there as regular men? My nails became claws, my teeth sharper than any vampire's fangs.

An instinct told me Kimaris's sensitivity lived in more places than his feet and his privates. My beast wriggled into his brain and pulled out the demon he punished himself with. I felt my face mold into the creature he'd encountered every time he slept, one devouring him night after night—whatever night meant to him.

I rose to my feet. My beast would protect me. My head reached the ceiling. My mouth hinged open. The part of me who was Charlotte tried not to gag, but if she had to tear Kimaris limb to limb and feast on his liver, so be it.

Kimaris fell to his knees and wrapped his arms over his head. "You don't scares me, girlie."

"Liar."

My breath scorched him and he whimpered. He crawled backward toward my closet, the skin beneath the bruising, pure white.

He sucked in his breath. "I cames to do a job. And I dids it. Abraxas gots what he wanted. You're one of us now, and I cans retire. I'm goings back to the pool and finish my pedi, and then I'm takings off to my own little island in the Caribbean. It's my reward."

He launched himself backwards and disappeared.

Mom's alarm went off. I panted like a dog. Slowly, my body shrunk to normal Charlotte size. My fangs raked over my lips as they pulled into my gums. My claws retracted.

I licked my lips, then bit down on my index finger hoping the pain would release the beast from my soul. I tried to think of the garden I'd seen when Ezequiel had held me, and how the voice promised me peace. The flow of the river, the gentle breeze, warm sunlight, Jesus playing golf and the voice whose essence was love—all of it seemed real. But now Ezequiel was probably being tortured.

Mom screamed in the kitchen. I took my time to get to her.

She slammed the telephone into the hook. "Some bastard called and said he saw Connie with Hayden at the Pioneer Club. He wouldn't give me his name. There's some prostitution ring, and Captain Hartman is involved in it with some Middle Eastern woman."

Mom had never said anything worse than "Oh, beans" or "Sugarfoot" in front of me. She rushed to her bedroom and came out three minutes later with her hair as wild as mine in the wrinkled dress she wore the day before. She forgot about her house shoes. They were still on her feet.

She grabbed her purse. "Stay here, Charlotte. Promise me you'll stay here."

My beast snarled. I coughed to cover it up. "I promise."

Why hadn't she noticed the Charlotte she'd given birth to had died? The beast was so much stronger. I *would* not hurt anymore. My beast would take care of me.

I stared at the floor until her car drove away. My beast needed feeding one way or the other. I pulled leftover macaroni and cheese from the fridge and shoved it into my mouth with my fingers.

The bell rang. I licked my fingers and opened the front door.

Abraxas stood there, dressed like the lawyers my government class had seen on a field trip to the city hall, in a neat black suit, a white shirt the color of his hair, and an elegant red tie. His cat eyes burned.

I wasn't surprised he showed up. "You've changed your outfit."

"All the better to blend in."

I leaned over and looked behind him. Yep, a black limo sat at the curb.

Abraxas held out his hand. "Shall we go?"

I accompanied him to the car like a dog on a leash. Halfway there, he stopped and looked up to a cloudless sky. The storm the night before seemed like an illusion.

He stretched his arms out as if to embrace my street. The temperature shot up by at least twenty degrees. I imagined the headlines on the nightly news about the record heat in Las Vegas and how quickly the mercury rose.

Abraxas opened one of the back doors. "After you, my dear."

I climbed in and sunk into a seat made of soft leather, though the luxuriousness of the limo barely registered. I stared blankly out the window as we traveled down my street and turned left. Outside, I knew the air smelled fresh and the skin of the sky was a brilliant blue, but my vision constricted. I looked through a dark tunnel. My beast saw nothing bright nor clean.

Abraxas patted my hand. "That's my girl. Everything has worked out. Lilith will be punished for her impudence. The angels will lose their foothold on Earth. Hell will permanently be sealed from Heaven."

What did he mean?

I honestly didn't care. I assumed we were on our way to Connie, but we turned down Rhonda's street instead. A throaty growl came out of my mouth.

Abraxas chuckled. "Patience, little demon."

The limo parked in Rhonda's driveway. Abraxas stepped out of the car and brushed lint from the sleeve of his jacket.

"Coming?"

Once again I followed.

He knocked at the door, and a few moments later Millie opened it. She looked like she'd aged five years.

"Mrs. Mildred Nelson?"

"Yes?"

He pulled out a badge from the inside pocket of his expensive coat. "I'm Detective Abraham Bannon. Do you know a man named Hayden Nelson?"

"He's my husband." She looked at me. "Charlotte, what are you doing here?"

"Charlotte's mother asked me to take care of her as Mr. Nelson was found with her sister."

Joe Friday would have been impressed with his lack of expression.

"Mr. Bannon, this is a bad time. My daughter—"

Abraxas flipped open a notebook and interrupted. "Rhonda?"

"How do you know her name?" Millie looked more agitated. "Did you tell this man her name, Charlotte?"

My beast hungered to tell a lie, but Abraxas answered. "Mrs. Nelson, has your daughter ever told you Mr. Nelson touched her inappropriately?"

Millie stood erect and frowned. "Hayden is a good man, Detective Bannon, and I resent you implying anything different. My daughter is in the hospital now, and I'm on my way to see her. This conversation is over." She almost closed the door but stopped herself. "Charlotte, you come with me."

A pang shot through me hearing about Rhonda. How it stabbed me. The Beast pounced on the feeling, ripping it apart, and I slid farther into darkness.

What did Rhonda matter? I stood mutely, feeling heat blast from Abraxas's body as he fed from Millie's anguish.

"Her mother wants her to stay with me."

Millie scoured my face.

Language had left me. I bent my head. My hair fell forward. I opened my mouth to let my beast shriek, but noise, like my life, was lost.

Abraxas put his hand on my shoulder and marched me back to the car.

Millie yelled at our backs. "I don't believe you're a cop. I'm calling the police."

"Be my guest." Abraxas didn't bother to look back at her. "I'm very pleased with you, Charlotte."

He crossed his legs when we were in the limo. His nails were beautifully manicured. I studied mine. Maybe I'd get a manicure one day.

"Behemoth had such potential. He did terrific work for thousands of years, yet it only took a girl who loved doughnuts to teach him about compassion. He believed he'd save her by betraying Ezequiel. And you." Smoke seeped from his ears, making rings the way smokers did in movies from the forties. "Ezequiel...such a future he would have had. You loved him, did you not?"

Despite the Beast's control over me, the answer was yes.

"Love, Charlotte, is our enemy. Remember that and you won't suffer the same fate as your brother and your friend."

I managed to croak out a few words. "Where ... are ...we ... going?"

"To innocent victims, Charlotte."

I gasped.

"Remember the paper you found about Hayden Nelson?"

I nodded.

"He actually tried to rescue Connie."

My heart broke once again. I hadn't died, not completely, but my head felt thick like I'd been drugged. I felt myself reach for some conclusion that kept eluding me, something to do with forgiveness.

We stopped at a traffic light.

"Look at me, Charlotte."

I tried to resist. I had to get out of the car and fight the beast, but that was impossible. As hard as I tried to stare through the window, my head turned toward him. The flames sparked in Abraxas's eyes, and I fell into pitch and ash. The worm, the jackal, and the beast awoke with fury.

Abraxas handed me a gun. "Your father's service revolver."

My three demons roared in triumph.

Contract

The limo traveled north, beyond the junkyards and the abandoned Hideaway Motel, a gray rectangle of cinder block surrounded by hard baked dirt. The highway divided expanses of flat wasteland, empty save for creosote bushes and the weight of the sun on the arid desert floor.

Abraxas pulled a different kind of communicator out of his pocket. A thin rectangle box fit in the palm of his hand. He read the details on the screen, using his right index finger to control it. I stared out the window, lulled by the monotonous scenery. An hour must have passed before the limo turned east onto an unmarked dirt road slowly descending into an arroyo cut with centuries of flash floods. Despite the rain the night before, dust billowed around us. The desert remained unquenchable.

A police car and my father's old Caprice blocked our way forward as the road had devolved into a narrow strip of silt. As we came to a stop, I wasn't surprised to see Connie and Mom fifty feet from us where the arroyo etched into a low bank of rubble.

Abraxas and I left the limousine and walked toward them. I felt as though I had no substance of my own. The weight of the gun kept me from peeling off the ground.

Connie looked like a working girl adorned in bright pink hot pants and a tight yellow shirt with sequins that cast dancing lights on the ground. Her ratted hair was stiff with too much Dippity Do. The woman who was once my mother held Connie in her arms.

Kimaris retirement loomed over them in his police commissioner's uniform, a bare foot on top of a man's neck who lay in the sand, his face turned in our direction. The rest of Kimaris's toenails were pink now.

Lily stood between him and the two other women, wearing the Levis and tee shirt she'd been in the night before. Her arms were splayed like a traffic cop, hands out signaling "Stop!"

Bad kitty.

Spasms shook me. I bent over, not able to control my laughter and dropped the gun.

Abraxas put a gentle hand on my back. "Pick it up, Charlotte."

He helped me stand. The gun calmed me.

My former mother moved her lips. Her free hand shielded her eyes from the sun, but she spoke to me. I almost felt sorry for her. She was incapable of appreciating my sinister glory with her human sensibilities of right and wrong.

I recognized Hayden's raw voice. He addressed Abraxas. "This lady found me at the Four Queens. Says her name is Lilith, and that she knew I was searching for Connie. I don't know who you are, but if you have any power over this goon tell him to let me up."

Kimaris pressed down and Hayden moaned. "How deliciously ironical you calls me a goon."

Hayden was a mortal schmuck among billions. Kimaris snorted with the mention of Lily's name.

Connie pulled away from Mom. "Lily found me and took me to Hayden's car. All Hayden tried to do was to take me home, but we were pulled over by the commissioner. He held his gun on us and made us get out. Then he called Mom on his radio and told her to meet us here."

Her attention turned to me. "Charlotte, what are you doing with that strange man?"

I didn't answer. I siphoned power from my demons. Any residue of Charlotte melted under the barrage of the sun. The gun delighted my hand.

Lily put her arms down. "We were trying to rescue Connie. Charlotte, you don't have to turn into who I used to be."

She had no idea the extent of her powerlessness.

Abraxas waved to Kimaris. "Step aside. I'll take it from here."

Kimaris snarled and took his revolver from his holster. "Shut up, Abraxas. I'm dones taking orders. Some vacation you gaves me. You promised me the Buccaneer Club and the whole island of Eleuthera, and what do I finds? An order back at Burning Sands to puts on this damn uniform again."

I felt nothing from being near Kimaris, no fear, not even anger. Charlotte had already died, so what did anything he might do matter? My own gun weighed me to the Earth and gave me substance. Without it, I'd become spirit, comfortable in my malignancy, grateful to no longer be human.

Kimaris rose to a full eight feet. "I'm taking outs this one before she becomes immortal. You don't knows what you created with her. First I'll deals with her, and then you and I are goings to have it out once and for all."

His shadow spread over Abraxas and me, though the sun hung in the wrong place to cast one. He stepped over Hayden. Mom and Connie rushed and helped him sit up. Connie's face turned white as she looked at the slime on her hands that had come from the back of Hayden's shirt.

"You ain't scarings me no more, Cupcake. I'm sending you to the moon."

Had he been watching old episodes of *The Honeymooners*? He raised his gun and aimed it at me.

Abraxas's voice became my conscience. "You're ready, Charlotte."

A cold confidence filled me. I was the girl of steel. I was Joan of Arc turned bad, more powerful than Kimaris's nightmares. I understood everything in a flash before Kimaris had a chance to pull the trigger. Abraxas could have bored a hole into the closet of any fourth grade girl who wanted go-go boots, but I desired them more than any other. My dad needed to feel good about himself, and Abraxas used his insecurities as bait. My sister offered herself as the vulnerable one. My mom would grieve far beyond anything she would ever show.

Abraxas had seen potential in me, but Kimaris's gut picked up on the real score. His brute instincts trumped Abraxas's smooth wiliness about the extent of my power.

Kimaris pulled the trigger, but this act reeked of nonsense. I imagined the bullet freezing in the rod, and so it did. I'd release it in my own good time.

A rustle filled the space the blast from the gun should have taken. Kimaris's shadow darkened, but then sequins seemed to have been poured over its curves, hemming it with white fire and rainbows.

Captain Hartman—or a being who sure looked like him—landed next to Lily. Angel wings don't have feathers, but are energy grids that pulsate into plumes of light. I now had the vision to ascertain this, a natural phenomenon, no more, no less.

Abraxas oozed contempt. "Michael, I expected you earlier."

Captain Hartman, Angel Michael, got to the point. "You're a liar. The barrier between Hell and Heaven has been breached, and you know it. We won't ever stop finding the alcoves where you think you've hidden yourself."

Abraxas laughed. "But Hide and Seek is such a fun game. And, reality is such a delight to wend and warp. So many permutations, Michael, that the On-High keeps having to redeem while I go about my play."

I'd had it with this conversation. I had a job to do, and if Abraxas believed the cards stacked up on his side, boy, was he in for a surprise. The mortals might as well have been a million miles away. For what I knew, they believed they witnessed a religious vision, the totality of light and darkness, beyond the veil of their understanding. A miracle mirage in the desert made Lily's appearance on the screen door almost laughable.

But wait—I was giving Mom and Connie too much credit. They didn't share my vision as they knelt with me in the Garcia's front yard. And they certainly didn't have the eyes to see that this woman had been shedding on the sofa for almost three years.

Lily wasn't fooled, of course. She stepped into the shadow-light next to Mr. Angel.

"Mr. *Arch*angel to you."

Damn it. Michael read my mind. He pulled a sword from his flowy angel dressy thing.

I let my demons rip. Charlotte became a speck with a memory not worth preserving. I took on the body of Kimaris's nightmare demon because I had to admit it was pretty impressive, but I added a variation of the helldog thing I learned about in school with my own three heads.

Lily crumbled to her knees. She began to pray. Shoot. Well, no matter, Michael was the one pissing me off.

"How dare you show your face here. I don't care how illuminated your holy visage shines, or that your light is the light from the On-High. I don't give a fuck. The only thing you've ever done is watch. You could have saved Daddy or helped Connie leave Freeman before he broke her heart. Did you ever try to convince Ezequiel he didn't need to stay in Hell? And now you show up like a big shot and think you're going to zap me with that sword. What good is good when it's so powerless?"

Captain Harman lowered the tip of his sword and scribbled something in the dirt. He glanced up. "Hello, Charlotte. You're still here."

Damn.

I started sobbing. My projections melted like they were cubes of ice lying beneath the September sun. Through the holy-profane-demonic mist Michael brought with him, I aimed the gun at Hayden.

In his suspended state, Kimaris groaned with muffled glee.

Abraxas stepped beside me. "Good girl. Him first."

I pulled back on the hammer, but Captain Hartman interrupted my concentration.

"You're absolutely right, Charlotte."

"Captain, you're annoying me."

Somehow calling him Michael didn't feel right, kind of like calling a teacher by his first name. If I didn't have the power to destroy him, I'd still blast him back to Kingdom Come.

"You asked for a guardian angel. I've been your witness, and I've done what I've been able to for you and your family. But, we angels aren't in the miracle department, at least 99 percent of the time. You humans must do the hard work."

"You're ticking me off big time. I'm not human anymore."

Lily walked through the mist. "Oh, baby, yes you are. You're gloriously human and divine and demonic. Free will sucks. But it's worth it in the long run, because—"

I was having none of this nonsense. "All will be well, and all manner of things will be well? I don't believe that."

Lily inched closer. "Michael used the 1 percent power he had to create a miracle so Abraxas picked Ezequiel to come to you, and he arranged for me to stay as close as possible after I changed. By the way, I detest the cheap Kitty Friskies your Mom has been buying lately."

"Don't listen to them, Charlotte." Abraxas voice was traced with anxiety.

My finger itched. I longed to experience what murder felt like. I might kill again and again, Hayden, Mom, Connie, myself. And I'd then hide away with Abraxas and be numb to everything but power. I always had a creative side. I'd draw the pictures, ones my Mom would absolutely hate, and he'd snap his fingers and make them real.

I might be five foot two for all eternity, but I'd be proud of it. I stood tall. "So, Michael." Using his name made me feel like a grown up. "You know who I am, right?"

"You're the Adversary,"

"You're darn tootin', I am."

Lily spoke to me as though she and I were alone, having a chat in my bedroom. "Charlotte, yes, you're the new Satan. The one who is also human. The one who is without myths to drag you down. The one who can clean things up."

Abraxas laughed. "I am the Satan."

Wrong, buster.

I might have been the one and only Satan, but I wasn't infallible. You see, with everything going on, I forgot about Kimaris and the bullet in his gun. He managed to wiggle out of suspended animation, even more pissed than before. Only now more at Abraxas than at me.

"That's what you think, Brother. I am goings to be the Big Guy."

The bullet whizzed by my ear, its punch accentuated with kinetic energy. Abraxas's screams filled the arroyo. Being shot didn't kill him, of course, but I bet he'd have a doozy of a headache.

Gabriel might have been flying around above because a loud horn blew so loudly the vibration made my body shake.

Michael had a pair of ethereal lungs on him because he shouted even louder than the alarm in the sky. "Charlotte, you have the key."

I did?

Connie broke through the mystical junk. She ran up to me and began to wrestle. "Drop the gun, stupid."

Surprised, I let it fly. Abraxas snapped it from midair.

"I love you, Charlotte." She slapped me. "What the hell are you doing?"

Connie had painted her eyelids with a shade of purple, even a stretch for her, but only one thing mattered. My sister was okay. I didn't even want to slap her back.

I looked at Michael. "By the key, you mean THE key?"

He nodded and tapped his head.

Abraxas and Kimaris were in a Mexican standoff, so focused on each other, their brotherly hate, made them blind. Blind to love.

I gathered myself. I had a lot of work to do, but I knew the first task at hand.

Michael raised his face to the sky, "Gabby, turned down the volume."

The sky quieted, and a hummed jet miles overhead. The people on board were going to see the biggest dust devil of their lives.

I took a deep breath the moment they fired at each other.

"ABRAXAS. KIMARIS. I CONDEMN YOU BOTH TO THE UNDERHELL."

And poof. A really, really huge poof, if I do say so myself. It registered a 6 on the Richter Scale.

I reached down and pulled off the go-go boots and flung them as far as my strength allowed into the desert. And then, to be on the safe side, so no other little girl would be lured by them, I made them go poof as well.

⤜⤜⤜ ⤛⤛⤛

When Mom, Connie, and I returned home, we found Bo in the recliner eating Pringles, watching Rocky and Bullwinkle. No horns or tail. He popped out of the chair.

"Charlotte, would you go outside with me for a minute?"

When the sliding glass door closed behind us, he took my hand.

"I'm sorry I ratted on you and Ezequiel to Abraxas, but I was desperate to save Rhonda. Abraxas told me he'd send Kimaris to the hospital to make sure she died."

He didn't say "Daddy Abraxas," but I had a hard time holding his hand. "You betrayed us because you love her?"

"It's complicated. Do you forgive me?"

I let go. "Not yet. But I'll think about it."

Maybe he did save Rhonda. Who knows? She was home now.

My boots poofing out of existence exorcised the three demons who'd ruined my life, but I was stuck in my funk. I went back to school, and in the next week the most dreadful thing I faced was P.E. first period. Though the metaphysical world of good and evil left me alone, I knew it would only be a matter of time before my life got complicated again.

And, of course, I worried about Ezequiel. About Daddy too. Bo didn't know what had happened to them. I didn't have the energy—and I mean this literally—to go "south" and investigate.

Poor Mom had no idea what to do about Connie. Millie suggested she let Connie be the free spirit her soul called her to be. She also announced she and Hayden were going on a belated Honeymoon trip to Mazatlan.

One evening we "young" people went to the Shakey's Pizza Parlor up on Boulder Highway. Jason and Connie got a booth for themselves. Their heads leaned toward each other in intense conversation. Connie had decided she wanted to follow the Grateful Dead and make macrame pot hangers for a living. Jason no doubt was trying to talk her out of it. He majored in Engineering.

What did he know about life?

Bo, Rhonda, and I sat around a large pepperoni pizza. Each of us ordered 7UPs. I might be the new Satan, but I didn't think I'd ever drink another Coke. Rhonda slowly ate bite by bite, pulling small chunks from her piece.

Bo frowned when she left the crust on her plate and put a new slice on it. "The Burning Sands is closing down. Did you hear?"

I nodded. "The news said a demolition crew is scheduled to blow it up in a month."

I didn't have to add that Archangel Captain Mike Hartman had been installed as the new police commissioner. They both knew.

On cue, Lily walked into the restaurant with Jesus and Archangel Mike, who carried an official looking notebook under his arm. Jesus went to the drink station. Mike and Lily joined us.

Lily had scratched at the door an hour before Jason and Rhonda picked us up. She hadn't offered any sympathy in her kitty guise the whole week, other than sitting on my homework and demanding to be petted.

Her beautiful non-demon self beamed. "How's it going?"

Mike set the notebook filled with Bo's beautiful script on the table.

I elbowed my brother. "Really?"

Bo smiled. "Well, I want to keep in practice."

I read CONTRACT upside down as Mike pointed to the word. Jesus carried three glasses of red wine, put them down and brought over a chair from the table next to us.

A big man in a crew cut jostled him. "Dirty hippie."

Jesus flashed him a peace sign and took a seat. "So, Charlotte, mind if we talk a little business?"

Oh, come on, Jesus, introductions first.

"Rhonda, this is Jesus. Jesus, this is Rhonda. I think you know Bo."

Rhonda took things in stride and held out her hand. "Can I tell Mom I met you?"

He reached across the table and held hers for a long moment. "I'd rather you didn't. At least not in the flesh."

Rhonda nodded and took a big bite from the new slice of pizza.

Lily sipped from her glass and set it down. "Charlotte, you need to understand what to expect with your new position."

I grew wary. "Like what?"

Mike must have had a background in law. "The first clause states you will live out your natural life until two thousand—"

I held my hand up. I used my Satie powers to stop him from filling in the last two digits of my lifespan.

Mike nodded. "Fair enough. Second clause. You will hold the power of good and evil within you. Free will dictates you must be tempted, but the more you right the wrongs in the universes, the easier it will be for you to harness the forces of light."

Jesus took a sip of wine and made a face. He let out a long sigh. "I did my best, Charlotte. The cosmological template is set for peace and justice and goodwill among men."

Rhonda corrected him. "Humans. Men and women."

"Right you are." Jesus pushed his glass away.

Lily leaned closer. "But, the old myths still hold power. Your job Charlotte is to become a part of them and change their fabric so that the human race grows up. We'll help you."

Bo whistled. "That'll take forever."

Rhonda peeled a pepperoni from her slice and popped it in her mouth. "Charlotte, you don't have to agree with this. Don't sign the contract."

My dear friend. She always knew me better than I did myself. My whole insides were shouting NO NO NO.

"I have free will, right?"

The three adults at the table nodded.

I had been contemplating my fate over the last week. I didn't want to seal the deal. Everyone might have been saved, but being in charge of waking up humanity made me queasy. Now I'd experienced power, I didn't want anything to do with it, other than having power over my own life.

"Then I relinquish my Satanhood."

Jesus broke into a smile. His upper front tooth was chipped. He had dimples. He took the contract from Mike and ripped it up. "Feel better?"

That easy? No wagging finger of the On-High hovering over our pizza?

A lightness filled my body. Ordinary human relief. "I feel great."

Mike choked on his wine, but Jesus patted his back until he caught his breath. "I'll clear it with Dad. Charlotte made the right decision." He pushed his chair back. "Charlotte, would you please come with me for a little stroll?"

Jason and Connie's platter had been pushed off to the side. They held hands and didn't pay attention when Jesus and I walked by. Jesus held the door for a family who were coming in, and then we stepped into the main room of Hell.

The ruts carved by the fire falls were full of wildflowers and the fiends and their towers had disappeared. Souls wandered around listlessly. If they had noticed, they would have seen no one guarding the elevator to the Purgatory Cafe. A free ride waited for everybody.

We made our way to Satan's apartment and found the door open. Daddy and Ezequiel sat in chairs in front of the Heaven window.

Jesus tapped on it and it dissolved. "Walt, ready to come aboard?"

Daddy lowered his head. "I am willing." He looked at me then. "Forgive me?"

I was honest. "As much as I can."

"Look after your mother and sister. And your brother."

He stood up, and I hugged him.

"The best I can. Goodbye, Daddy."

I was ready to let him go.

Jesus took Daddy's hand, and they stepped into Heaven.

Before the window took substance again, Jesus pointed to me. "Ezequiel, get her back home, okay?"

"Of course, Boss."

We were alone. I asked only one thing. "Where are your wings?"

I took Ezequiel's hands and pulled him from the chair. His wings, those bright pulsing plumes of energy, expanded for a moment. Then he collapsed them back into himself so I wouldn't be blinded.

"You've left me with a lot to do, Charlotte."

"Are you mad at me?"

Ezequiel's lips moved into something less than a grin. "Never. I owe you. You saved my soul."

We wrapped our arms around each other and didn't talk for a long while. I lifted my head and he kissed me. I felt fully alive, and allowed the pain of knowledge to fill me. We might not see each other for an Eternity.

"You won't be visiting, will you?"

"I can't. I don't want to drag any of what I have to deal with into your life. You go and be Charlotte. Be at peace without Hell haunting you ever again."

"I think Joanne's forgiven you."

"I know my sister has."

We played a couple games of blackjack and talked for a long time. And then, like waking from a dream, I had a glass of 7UP in my hand. Lily and Mike were gone, but the three wine glasses were left on the table.

Bo and Rhonda broke from a kiss.

Rhonda pushed her empty plate away.

I swirled the ice at the bottom of my glass. "It's time for us to all go home."

Acknowledgments

Cover design by Kate Rauner. Images from *kickassrenderstock.com*

Author photo by Eve West Bessier

C. Austin, Miles, *Come to the Garden Alone* (Public Domain)

I dedicate this book to my Borderland Writers Co-Op partners, Kate Rauner, Kris Neri, and EJ Randolph. These three women are amazing writers and friends who have given me hours of feedback and writing suggestions. My writing and personal life has been enriched by knowing these wonderful women.

About the Author

Thank you for reading *Charlotte and the Demons*. This is a work of love, resurrected from a manuscript I started in 2004. Charlotte is a spunkier version of myself as a girl, but then my closet didn't open to Hell. I lived in Anaheim, not in Las Vegas, but both cities have their elements of magic. I know there are upsetting things in this book. Al Anon and other Twelve Step groups are available in most places. Please make contact if you feel you need support. Suicide prevention hotlines are as close as your favorite search engine. The world needs you!

My other novels are *Hungry* (HarperCollins), *Starved*, and *Whispers of the Old Ones*.

I worked as a reading specialist for most of my years as an educator. I live in Silver City, New Mexico with my husband, Bill, an Australian Shepherd named Sparky, and a Mackerel Tabby, Jinxy Cat.

Reviews are love. I would greatly appreciate your leaving a review on Amazon. I can't stress how important these are for authors. Even a one-liner would be a wonderful gift. Also, if you enjoyed Charlotte's story, please tell your friends about it.

Made in the USA
Monee, IL
26 February 2023

28053754R00143